David Tristram is n̲   ̲ ̲ ̲ ̲ ̲ ̲ ̲ most popular comedy playwrights. Every single night, on average, there are at least two of his plays being performed somewhere in the world - sometimes in far flung places like New Zealand, the Vanuatu Islands in the South Pacific, Mexico, Argentina, or Dar Es Salaam.

In this, his first novel, he brings his trademark hilarity to every page, but through the medium of a highly unusual and poignant story.

Stage Plays by David Tristram

The Opposite Sex

What's For Pudding?

Inspector Drake's Last Case

Unoriginal Sin

Inspector Drake & The Time Machine

The Secret Lives of Henry & Alice

Brenton Versus Brenton

Forget-Me-Knot

Inspector Drake & The Perfekt Crime

Last Tango In Little Grimley

Ghost Writer

A Jolly Sinister Jape

The Extraordinary Revelations of Orca The Goldfish

Last Panto In Little Grimley

Joining The Club

Cinders, The True Story

The Fat Lady Sings In Little Grimley

Sex, Drugs & Rick'n'Noel

A Bolt From The Blue

For more information on Flying Ducks Publications
visit the website:

www.flyingducks.biz

A BOLT FROM THE BLUE

David Tristram

Flying Ducks Publications

A Flying Ducks paperback

First published in Great Britain

by

Flying Ducks Publications

2005

ISBN 1-900997-06-1

978-1-900997-07-2

Printed in Great Britain by
Antony Rowe Ltd., Chippenham, Wiltshire

www.flyingducks.biz

Why I wrote this book

I was determined never to write a novel, and here it is.

You'd think that, having published around twenty plays in as many years, dashing off a quick novel would be easy meat. Not so.

I like a challenge as much as the next man. In fact, I've often been accused of having a rather over-active competitive streak, so in theory I should like a challenge more than the next man. But nevertheless I always steered well clear of the novel. It's simply something that I always said I wouldn't do – I even wrote a list of reasons why I shouldn't, or couldn't, and I intend to share those with you now.

The first reason was the sheer scale of the work involved. I was told that the average short novel contains around 60,000 words, give or take. I quickly realized that I didn't even know 60,000 words, let alone have the ability to arrange them into something worthy of taking up a reader's valuable time. I later discovered to my great relief that you are allowed to use some words twice – in fact some of the more common words, such as 'the' or 'and' may crop up several times in a novel. Nevertheless, it's still a lot of words to a playwright. A typical stage play is more like 10,000 words, which is far more in scale with my work ethic.

i

The second reason I've always shied away from novels in the past is that, if you're going to jeopardize so many trees to tell a story, you really need 'the big idea'.

"What's the big idea?" I hear you asking. Well, in short, it's one worthy of all the pomp and circumstance of parading your book in printed form in the hope that someone like yourself will pluck it from the shelf and take a peek. It's been pretty tough getting this far, and your time is precious, so the last thing I'm going to do is drag you from your friends, family, TV, the beach and other worthy distractions just to tell you some half-baked tale about a man who takes his dog for a walk, or mows his lawn. So I decided to bide my time and wait for the big idea, which I confidently predicted would never come.

The third reason I gave myself for not writing a novel was that it would distract me from writing plays, which I already spend too little of my time doing. This was a pretty good excuse, I thought, and would take some cracking.

There's a novel in all of us, so the old saying goes. If that's true, then I wasn't sure where mine was hiding, but I was quite content to let it stay there - in fact not just content, as I say, but positively determined.

And then, it happened.

Just from nowhere, out of a clear blue sky, it hit me, like a bolt from the blue. The big idea.

With one of my main excuses for not writing a novel now totally blown away, I quickly looked to the other two for emotional comfort and support. Unfortunately, they started crumbling before my very eyes. Suddenly, with a big idea to play with, 60,000 words didn't seem quite so daunting after all, especially if I'm allowed to repeat some of my favourites.

The final excuse, that all this work would distract me from writing plays, seemed like it would hold firm, until I suddenly realized that the big idea was big enough to sustain both a novel and a stage play, and that writing one might help me finish the other.

Bugger.

In a mild panic, I invented one last new excuse. I decided to hide behind the belief that I simply wasn't up to the task. I couldn't do the idea justice, I concluded, so let it go. But then that old vicious competitive streak kicked in, the demons entered my head, and I was helpless to resist.

So here it is. The novel I'll never write. Whether the idea was big enough, of course, and whether I was or wasn't up to the task, only you can tell.

But please, don't count the words.

Carpe Diem
Make your lives extraordinary.

Keating

CHAPTER ONE

Edward Jones was eating a ham sandwich when he was struck by lightning.

The details, unfortunately, are a little sketchy. Edward was the only first-hand witness and, just as a mischievous spark of static can erase vital data from a floppy disk, so 150,000 volts jolting up the spine of an unsuspecting victim can have a definite fogging effect on the memory. Nevertheless, through a combination of second-hand testimony and logical assumption, we can piece together most of the facts.

First of all, it was definitely ham. Edward always had ham on a Friday, and his wife, Mary, later confirmed that she had packed four rounds of Sainsbury's finest. We even know the sandwich was in his left hand (charred remnants were later chiseled from Edward's grip) and the probability is that his right hand was occupied with a copy of the Daily Mail crossword. Edward usually tackled the crossword in his lunch break, though no physical evidence of the newspaper remained.

We also know that the time was 1.07pm - the time that the glass on Edward's watch face had melted onto the dial, encapsulating the fingers. The only other salient fact is that, at the time of impact, Edward was suspended sixty feet in the air, strapped to an electricity pylon.

It was not unusual for Edward to be strapped to an electricity pylon. He spent most of his working life either up a pylon, down a pylon, or driving to another pylon. The utilities company for whom he'd worked for over fifteen years sent him all around the country performing routine maintenance tasks. On this particular occasion, he was in the process of mending a connector which had been badly damaged during a violent storm on the previous evening.

The connector had, in fact, been struck by lightning.

Now, there's an old saying about lightning, the gist of which is that it tends not to re-visit old haunts. Just Edward's luck, then, that he was in the vicinity of a bolt which was determined to buck the trend. But what made the incident even more bizarre was the fact that, as Edward leant back to examine his lunch, perfectly trusting the integrity of the leather harness which held him high above the Shropshire countryside, he began whistling. And he did that because he was enjoying one of nature's wonders - a beautiful summer's day. The birds were twittering, the butterflies were fluttering, the sheep were grazing, the sun was casting its golden glow on the cornfields. Not even a breath of wind.

It seems that Edward was hit with, quite literally, a bolt from the blue.

The local farmer was the first on the scene. He'd heard the bang well above the deafening clatter of his antiquated tractor, and had turned just in time to see a smouldering figure plummeting from the pylon at the edge of his field. Also at the end of his field was an enormous mound of freshly dumped manure.

The involuntary skydiver disappeared with a muted squelch.

There's no doubt that the manure would have helped break the fall. It's also possible that it may have had a beneficial cooling effect on Edward's charred skin. But it did nothing to encourage any would-be rescuer.

The farmer made a few anxious calls, and then cautiously circled the mound, listening for muffled cries, and waiting for back-up. The fire brigade were the first to respond. Then the paramedics. Then a curious passer-by stopped to ask what was happening, followed by another, and soon there was a small but enthusiastic crowd of spectators, who watched proceedings from a respectful distance, carefully balancing the needs of eye and nose. Last to arrive on the scene were the local First Responders, who to their embarrassment had only found out about the emergency when they

3

arrived home from their first-aid course.

The Fire Chief took control, taking a few anxious minutes to assess the situation. It was far from straightforward. This was one hell of a pile of shit. From sixty feet, and in total freefall, Edward's progress into the mound had been irresistible. His body had drilled a path deep into its steaming core.

Winching him back through the human-shaped plughole was a non-starter. Too much suction. Besides, someone that exact shape would have had to follow him in with a rope, and then find the elbow room to attach it. And there was a distinct shortage of volunteers. Digging him out seemed to be the only answer.

So, after a military style briefing, involving much chuntering and serious noddings of heads, the farmer's antiquated hardware was seconded by the Fire Chief, and a small army of dedicated professionals started nibbling round the edges of the steaming mound with shovels.

It was a hot day. You could cut the atmosphere with a knife. No-one was seriously expecting to pull Edward from the manure alive and, as the charred and stinking body was eventually unearthed, the paramedic on standby to give mouth-to-mouth was keeping his fingers crossed that it wasn't even a close call. So you can imagine everyone's surprise when Edward suddenly sat bolt upright and gasped.

His face was completely black, except for two

white ovals where his glasses had been. And one of his eyebrows was missing. He looked like a startled raccoon. Or is it a negative of a raccoon? Either way, it was a raccoon with one eyebrow. Smoke was gently twirling from the spiked ends of his hair, and his left-hand was clutching a ham toasty.

He gazed slowly up towards the pylon. His leather safety harness, still dangling from the top of the structure, was on fire. Three feet below, partially melted onto a metal strut, stood a pair of rubber safety boots, drooping like a pair of chocolate Wellingtons in front of a log fire.

Then, with the assembled spectators watching in stunned silence, Edward gave a curious faint smile, hic-coughed, and passed out.

Now, it's worth taking a few moments here to cover the obvious anomaly. There are, of course, those (and you may be amongst them) who can't help thinking that when a man mending an electricity pylon suddenly gets fried to a cinder on a pleasant summer's day, it's a decent bet that the pylon was responsible, rather than any rogue bolt of lightning. And yes, on the face of it, that's where the smart money would go. But, tempting as the theory is, the facts don't appear it bear it out.

For a start, we have the evidence of the utility company, who say that if proper procedures were followed, such an accident would have been impossible. And then we have Edward's own impeccable safety record - fifteen years up pylons and not so much as a tingle. What's more, the

Health & Safety Executive investigation was immediate and thorough, and found no evidence of human error or company negligence. And then we have the testimony of eighty-two year-old George Daniels, the nearest we have to an eye-witness, who swears that he saw a blinding flash of forked lightning crackle through the skies at around lunchtime when he was out walking his dog, Gerald.

The controversy still rages today. Some simply won't buy the lightning theory at any price. Others question the testimony of anyone strange enough to call a dog Gerald.

But, in a sense, it's all irrelevant. The fact is, Edward Jones was electrocuted, and no-one argues that, on the eve of his fortieth birthday, he had cheated death in the most spectacular fashion. But whatever the cause, everyone agrees that this is when it all began. This is the day that the process was put inexorably into motion. And, though no-one realized it at the time, this was the beginning of the events which were eventually to make Edward Jones the most extraordinary and famous man on the planet.

CHAPTER TWO

The first thing Edward saw when he regained consciousness was a ham sandwich.

"I've brought you some food, love - in case they weren't feeding you right."

Edward's bleary raccoon eyes gradually pulled focus from the sandwich, foreground, to his wife's face, some three feet behind. She smiled, blandly. "How are you feeling?"

Excellent, he thought. Never better.

As he slowly opened his mouth to respond, he felt his top lip split like a fat man's trousers. A small bead of bright red blood popped out, and moistened his tongue. That's if it was his tongue. It felt like a badly barbecued sausage. He had to make every word count.

"Where am I?"

"You're in hospital, love. One of your eyebrows is missing."

Edward wondered if this was more a job for the

police, rather than doctors, but was in no mood to quibble. He didn't know how it was possible to feel so numb and yet hurt so much. He continued his no-nonsense pursuit of the facts.

"What happened?"

"You were electrocuted."

The curt and improbable explanation instantly offended Edward's professional pride. Fifteen years up pylons and not once had he put a foot wrong. Just as well, really, as putting a foot wrong up pylons tended to result in revising most of your future plans. Mary could see in his facial reaction that Edward was wounded by the suggestion - even, dare I say it, shocked - so she quickly added that he had been struck by lightning, by way of comforting him.

Edward struggled to come to terms with the information. He didn't remember much about the incident, but subliminal fragments started flashing through his mind, like images from a crude flick book animation. A red tractor in a field. A ham sandwich. A butterfly. A harness on fire. Melted safety boots. A sense of blackness, and warmth. A strange smell. He couldn't visualize the smell, but he could smell it all right. Long after he'd lost the image of the butterfly, he'd remember that smell.

A junior doctor, who looked as if he hadn't slept for a fortnight, arrived at the bedside to go through the usual junior doctor ritual of looking quizzically at a clipboard, then at his watch, then back to the clipboard to deposit a biro scribble that no-one, including the junior doctor, would ever again be able to decipher. Without once attempting to make eye contact with his patient, he then fought to control an enormous gaping yawn which threatened to dislocate the top of his head, before scuttling off to the next bed to repeat whole procedure. Edward found it all faintly depressing. When he was younger, he had always considered doctors to be granite figures of authority. He noted with dismay that this one looked about thirteen. It was one of the classic signs of his steadily advancing years, of course - policemen were also starting to look like grammar school boys in fancy dress. These days only judges seemed to have the necessary maturity to command his respect, but then they usually blew it by wearing wigs, having ridiculously pompous voices, displaying outlandish amounts of nose-hair, and generally not knowing who David Beckham or The Beatles were.

Mary waited in hushed reverence until the doctor was out of earshot.

"You were very lucky, they reckon."

Really? Being electrocuted and landing in a pile of shit was not everyone's idea of luck.

"Anyway - seeing as how you missed it, best open this now. Happy birthday, love."

Mary handed Edward a card and a small, wrapped present. He suddenly remembered it was the big one tomorrow - forty. It was tomorrow, wasn't it?

9

What did she mean, missed it? He decided to push that thought out through his crackle-glazed lips.

"What do you mean - missed it?"

"It was your birthday yesterday. I wanted to give you your present then, but the doctors said best not disturb you - as you were unconscious."

"Yesterday? You mean I've been out for three days?"

"Near enough. Go on, then. Open it."

Edward looked down at the small present. The very small present. No more than a few inches long, barely half an inch wide, and soft to the touch. What had she bought him? An eyebrow?

His stiff and blackened fingers struggled to unravel the uninviting parcel. It looked like it had been wrapped by a small child in a big hurry. Finally, more in frustration than excitement, he managed to tear off enough of the over-sellotaped outer to pluck out the contents.

It was a something - a small something - wrapped in red tissue paper. Faced by yet more irritating sticky tape around its middle, Edward opted to rip a small hole in the side of his paper cracker and feed the mystery object out through it. He managed to reveal a glint of metal - just enough to grasp between thumb and forefinger. That's if it was his thumb and forefinger. They could be another couple of cremated sausages. One of them might even be his tongue. He squeezed. He pulled. And there it was. A tie-clip.

"It's a tie-clip," added Mary helpfully. "I always said you needed one."

It's true. She always had said that. The fact that Edward had never agreed was a mere detail. The fact that Edward never wore ties might also, you'd have thought, been a minor consideration.

Now, before we proceed to make judgments, a few words about this tie-clip. It was made of eighteen carat gold - custom-made, in fact - in a sort of opened scroll shape, and engraved with Edward's name across the front in a richly ornate typeface. It cost over a hundred pounds. So, as tie-clips go, it was up there with the best of them.

But even though this tie-clip may have entered our story in the guise of a gift, we all know that its real purpose is as a metaphor - a metaphor for the fact that all was not well with the Jones' marriage.

Put simply, whereas Edward couldn't think of anything he'd like less for his fortieth birthday than a tie-clip, Mary couldn't think of anything better. That was the difference between them. Small, but significant.

When they'd married some nineteen years previously, they had no doubt seen eye to eye on a number of things - the state of the nation; the colour of the lounge wallpaper; their own particular manifestation of easy-listening music; flared jeans; a mutual dislike of Aunty Joan, dogs, cats and people who smoked; an appetite for curries - but over the years it had all slowly faded into irrelevance. What they shared now was physical space - a series of rooms - but mentally they occupied different planets.

Not that there was any major conflict. They still both disliked Aunty Joan, but other than that they chugged along like two trains on parallel tracks - both owned by the same operating company, both displaying the same logo, both sheltering overnight in the same depot, but never likely to touch bumpers. They were Mr and Mrs Jones, with all the passion, mystery and excitement that that implies.

"Well? Do you like it?"

Edward wanted with all his soul to say that it was the tackiest and most life-denuding piece of shite he'd ever had the misfortune to clap his raccoon eyes on. But, as usual, he put his soul on hold, and struggled to find a politician's answer.

"It's very…shiny."

"It's gold. Eighteen carat."

"That would account for it, then."

"Try it on."

The conversation had reached new levels of absurdity. How was he expected to try on a tie-clip wearing a hospital gown? He was now more convinced than ever that his wife of nineteen years had mislaid what sketchy fragments of a plot she once followed. He decided to tell her straight that she was off her trolley and he'd had enough.

"Maybe later."

"All right, love. If you're tired."

"Yes, I am tired. And my tongue feels like a sausage."

"Oh, I'm sorry love. I've only brought you the ham."

"No, I meant…"

Never mind. It wasn't worth it.

"Oh, you haven't opened your card!"

"Oh. Would you mind? Only my fingers…"

Edward watched in awe as Mary opened the card, smiling as she studied its cover, and then silently read the verse to herself.

"Ah! How lovely!" she said, as if she hadn't chosen it herself and was seeing it for the first time. "Do you want to look?"

The next few seconds would be tricky. Edward had to feign a benign facial reaction, regardless of how monstrously banal the imagery now laid before him.

He prepared himself for the worst, and found himself under-prepared.

The cover of the card featured a large-eyed puppy dog cradled in a basket of flowers, and the words "To My Husband, With All My Love" in a typeface and colour combination which could only have been masterminded by the genius behind My Little Pony. It was the greetings card equivalent of a pink bouffant poodle. The verse inside, which would probably have been rejected as overly sentimental by the late Barbara Cartland, visibly made Edward wince. Mary interpreted this positively, thinking he'd been touched, which in a manner of speaking he had.

"Well - what do you think?"

Edward needed a masterpiece of political rhetoric. But as his lips parted, his mind went blank. His desiccated sausage of a tongue glued itself to the back of his top teeth, as if to say "I'm not getting you out of this one, pal." Mary's eyes widened in anticipation.

For Edward, passing out now seemed the only dignified option. But he was saved by a timely intervention by a cultured, authoritative voice.

"I see you're back with us, Mr Jones."

Edward looked up, and then up some more. The tallest man in the world stood by his bedside, the sort that could pat basketball players on the head while keeping his arms by his side. He was wearing a shabby old brown tweed suit, check shirt and mustard tie. Or was that just a lot of mustard down his tie? He looked about sixty, frail and thin as a stick insect, but with a face full of knowledge. Now this was a *real* doctor.

"Edward, I'm Mr Rogers, the consultant. You had us worried for a while. Mind if I take a look around?"

"Help yourself."

He yanked shut the curtains around the bed and began prodding at Edward with his stethoscope, front and back. Mary sat like a timid mouse, not daring to squeak. Mr Rogers leaned right into Edward's face, and stared deep into his raccoon eyes.

All Edward could see was the doctor's enormous, bushy eyebrows, which dominated the immediate landscape. They were truly magnificent specimens, like a pair of exotic caterpillars from Papua New Guinea or the Cayman Islands. Perhaps Edward was just jealous. What he wouldn't give for just one of those eyebrows.

With a flourish and seemingly from nowhere, the doctor produced a miniature torch, which he proceeded to shine deep into Edward's pupils at point-blank range. The surreal white light, set against the soundtrack of the doctor's hushed, confidential instructions, made Edward feel strangely drowsy and compliant, as if he were under the spell of a master hypnotist.

"Look up….down…straight ahead. Any pain?"

"Yes."

"Anywhere in particular?"

"Just the body."

"How's your memory, Edward?"

"Okay I think, Doctor er…"

"…Rogers, if you recall. Pop your tongue out for me. Mmm. Oh dear. I wouldn't put that back into your mouth if I were you."

The doctor snapped off his torch like a hypnotist snapping his fingers, and Edward instantly came round. With his first conscious act, he found himself slipping a birthday card under his pillow as the doctor wheeled around to finally acknowledge Mary.

"And you must be Mrs Jones."

"Oh, yes, doctor!"

She addressed him as she would any royalty, pope or world leader.

"Well, your husband's had a very lucky escape. I'm going to hang on to him for another day or so, if that's all right - then we'll see what we can do about getting him home."

"Thank you, doctor."

"Just drink plenty of water, and rest."

"I will, doctor."

"No, I'm talking to Mister Jones now."

"Oh, sorry doctor."

And with that, the two exotic caterpillars turned and disappeared through the curtains.

"That was the consultant, Mr Rogers," said Mary, as if it were a vital secret no-one else was allowed to hear.

"I know. He said."

"He came to see you yesterday. But you were unconscious."

"That's probably why I didn't recognize him."

"I phoned Martin, but he can't get here until Thursday."

Martin was the one tangible thing Edward and Mary had in common, apart from their living quarters and their lively views on tie-clips. Their son of eighteen summers was conceived on their wedding night. We can calculate this with some certainty, as their next attempt at love-making was three months later, which would have made Martin's birth premature. It would be undignified to go into detail here, but clearly the maiden voyage hadn't gone down a storm with either party. It did, however, bear fruit, and Martin's general presence over the next few years provided sufficient distraction and common purpose to hold the couple together, when all logic said they should be apart.

So what attracted them in the first place? Well, in a nutshell, Edward had married Mary on the rebound - actually, not just on the rebound, but on the rebound with a capital OTR.

He'd been outrageously in love with a girl called, bizarrely enough, Mary. Not the current Mary, of course. Oh, no. Altogether a different Mary. A Mary who was dark, wild, passionate, witty, tantalizing, sensuous, and devastatingly feminine. Edward loved every crevice of her personality, and the packaging it came in. He loved her laugh. He loved her temper. He loved her unpredictability. At least he did, until she unpredictably ran off with a Hell's Angel called Craig.

Craig had earned his gang name - Craig the Con - by virtue of being an ex-convict. He had been detained at Her Majesty's pleasure for seven years after accidentally murdering a rival biker. The official conviction cited manslaughter, his lawyer having done a nifty bit of footwork in persuading the twelve good men and true that Craig hadn't actually meant to kill his opponent, merely scare him a little, when he repeatedly ran over his face with his Harley Davidson. It went heavily in his favour with the jury that the victim, Jimmy the Slash, was an even more delightful piece of work than Craig, and few would mourn his passing.

The sight of this fun-loving leather-clad murderer presumably stirred some deep animal instinct in Mary. She immediately booked her mid-life crisis early to avoid disappointment, and disappeared on the back of Craig's Harley, never to be seen in civilized company again.

Edward was mortified. He even considered picking a fight with Craig, but was persuaded by his friends that he would then be mortified in a more literal sense. Those same friends - we needn't trouble you with their names here - took Edward to the local pub and set about bathing his mental wounds with obscene quantities of lager.

In walks Mary II, with mousey friend. Edward is

drunk, and rebounding from a heavy relationship at warp factor nine. Mary is shy, relatively plain, and just at that stage of her life where she's beginning to wonder if she should re-decorate the shelf and make it her permanent home.

Edward thought he'd found a Mary substitute, conveniently called Mary - but one who wouldn't run off with a tattooed rebel - and almost before he had time to sober up he was down the aisle with a carnation and putting a deposit on a small but tidy semi in the suburbs.

Then came Martin - not exactly planned.

Mary's parents, and therefore Mary, had rather old-fashioned views on pre-marital sex and so, even though it wasn't a particularly long courtship, by the time Edward got Mary anywhere near a duvet he was like a ravenous coyote with dangerously high blood pressure.

With the wedding disco's final Lionel Ritchie number still ringing in his ears, Edward ushered Mary brusquely up the hotel corridor to the bridal suite, grappled maniacally with several hundred key card and door handle combinations to effect entry, and without even stopping to switch on the lights proceeded to suck on whatever fleshy bits of his new bride were currently available.

Mary's traditional white wedding dress, which made her look like a gigantic shuttlecock, was secured with a complex arrangement of hooks and eyes, poppers, hidden fasteners, mortise locks and infra-red sensors, and it proved more than a match for Edward's fumbling hands. In desperation, he finally opted for trying to yank it over her head, where it got hopelessly entangled in some equally complex arrangement of hairpins, tiaras, necklaces and ear-rings.

The shuttlecock was now inside out, and Mary's head and arms were nowhere to be seen. But no matter. He'd found the bits he was after. Besides, he'd seen the head before, and it was nothing to get excited about. In an ideal world, Edward would have done the gentlemanly thing and asked Mary to join him, but it seemed nothing short of having her head shaved could liberate her now, and women are fussy about their hair.

To the soundtrack of muffled female shrieks and male coyote howls, and lit only by the sickly yellow glow of the halogen car park lamp outside the bedroom window, the final few moments of the tender love scene were played out.

Both were inebriated to the point where it was tricky to work out which limb belonged to which body, especially with one of the heads missing, and the resultant lack of finesse left Mary shy of further attention for some considerable period. To be fair, at Mary's muffled insistence, Edward did use a condom, but when the newly-weds finally regained consciousness the next day they found it firmly attached to Mary's toe, where it was unlikely to do its best work.

For the next eight months, virtually daily, Mary

was throwing up. All in all, she was not entirely won-over by the whole love-making act. On the one subsequent occasion that she was persuaded by Edward to let him have another stab at it, if that's the expression I want, it only served to remind them both why it hadn't been a total hit with the viewers last time.

So, then there was Martin. The name was Mary's idea - after her father, whose name was Martin. Edward wanted to call him, well, anything but Martin, but he let it go. He let everything go. He hated himself for being so weak. In darker moments, he wanted to tell her all about the other Mary. He even toyed with becoming a Hell's Angel himself, but he didn't look good in leather, and was scared of motorbikes.

For the next eighteen years, Martin was the focal point of the Jones' household. Everything else had to take a back seat - fun, conversation, tidiness, wealth - as Martin the baby progressed to become Martin the toddler, Martin the brat, Martin the nightmare teenager, and latterly Martin the sailor. Having sucked all the life out of his parental home, Martin had jumped ship and joined the Navy as soon as was old enough to shave, leaving an emotional vacuum of epic proportions.

Joining the Navy had been Martin's dream ever since he'd first thought about it two weeks earlier. Inspired by images of Tahitian beauties placing garlands round his neck and having a woman in every port, Martin signed up for the full eighteen years, only to discover that he would spend the first three in a dry-dock classroom in Portsmouth.

This had, to use a convenient seafaring analogy, knocked the wind out of his sails somewhat, and he was now in the process of trying to leave the Navy and pursue a more level-headed career as a rock star.

Martin was young, and simply yearned for adventure. But had he known what extraordinary adventures were about to unfold in his own family home - events involving eminent scientists, the world's spiritual and political leaders, the entire news media and awesome, mind-boggling sums of money, he would probably have stayed right where he was.

CHAPTER THREE

Having hinted at mysterious happenings in Chapter One, and then promised adventure beyond imagination at the end of Chapter Two, you're probably expecting Chapter Three to start with a real bang. Enough background info, I hear you saying, on with the show.

So no doubt you'll be a tad disappointed to learn that, for a very long while, nothing happened.

I say nothing - there were perhaps one or two minor developments worthy of note. The exotic caterpillars wriggled in to see Edward again a few days later, and were amazed by his progress. He was still badly charred, of course, but it was nothing a good session with a Brillo pad wouldn't sort out, and his heart, blood pressure and all other vital signs were as steady as a rock. So, he was released from hospital the same day, with a note suggesting that he refrained from electrocuting himself for at least a fortnight, after which he could return to duty. That was on the Wednesday afternoon.

The prodigal son Martin arrived from Portsmouth on compassionate leave to visit on the Thursday morning, as planned, because neither parent had remembered to update him. He was directed to the appropriate ward by a nurse who'd only just come back on duty and wasn't yet au fait with the latest releases. Martin found an empty bed, and assumed the worst.

To compound matters, still hanging on the end of the bed was the clipboard labelled 'Jones' which, when viewed in haste upside down by an anxious offspring, showed a graph suggesting Edward had gone downhill fast and then flat-lined.

Martin rushed home to comfort his mother, only to find the barbecued but otherwise healthy remains of his father sitting in the armchair, watching the midday news on television. With the resultant outburst of relief and emotion that always follows such moments, Martin bollocked his dad fiercely for causing him such worry, hugged his mom briefly, handed her his washing, and went to the pub to catch up with old mates.

Then, as I say, nothing happened. Edward scrubbed himself clean, re-grew his eyebrow, and went back to climbing pylons. Mary went back to making ham sandwiches every Friday. Martin went back to the Navy, putting in a request to join the regimental band on bass guitar. Everything was as it was.

For five whole years.

Even then, what happened next didn't get off to a particularly dramatic start. Were this book ever to be made into a film, what happened next wouldn't be one of those full orchestra shock staccato stab with crash zoom camera moments which make the cinema audience gasp and jump. It might - just might - make it to be one of those slightly eerie solo violin sustained single note gentle de-focus moments which leave the audience thinking 'Something a bit weird's just happened but I don't know what it was.'

The moment in question occurred at 7.35pm, on Edward's forty-fifth birthday. To celebrate, Mary had arranged for him to take her out for a meal, and Edward was just adding the finishing touches to his half-hearted attempt to get ready. He was dutifully wearing the new suit Mary had chosen for him, the new shirt, tie and other carefully selected tie-clip accessories, and was about to walk out of the bedroom when something – he wasn't sure what – compelled him to have a sneaky look at his bald patch.

Edward had first noticed his bald patch when he was thirty-five. Again we can pin down the date and time with some certainty - October 19th, 4.25pm. He'd just had some mirror wardrobes fitted in the bedroom, and was testing how smoothly the doors slid in their tracks when he happened, entirely by accident, to find the right angle to catch sight of the back of his head in the dressing table mirror behind.

Edward wasn't a particularly vain man, but the sudden realization that he had a distinct bald spot came as a bit of a shock, though obviously as shocks go it wasn't in the same league as the lightning incident.

At regular intervals over the next few days, Edward obsessively double-checked and triple-checked his findings from every angle using a hand mirror - even at one stage employing a Polaroid camera, the results of which looked like early pictures of the moon.

Having finally confirmed that the hole in his hairzone layer was much bigger than first feared, he went deep into denial. What he couldn't see, he reasoned, wouldn't hurt him, so from then on he avoided mirrors altogether, other than simple cursory front-on glances to make sure there were no foreign objects attached to his teeth or nose.

But this day, at this moment, something deep within urged him to take another look. Perhaps it was the passing of another age milestone. But why? He'd had nine other birthdays since and not even been tempted.

He caught sight of the hand mirror on the dressing table, and before he'd had time to think he found himself dangling it above his head and staring intently into the mirror wardrobe door to locate its reflection.

What he saw both puzzled and strangely excited him. The bald patch, if you could call it that, had virtually gone. The three-inch wasteland which he had once charted in cartographic detail, and which he fully expected to have spread to the size of a saucer in the intervening decade, had reduced to the merest hint of thinning hair around his crown.

Cue eerie sustained violin note.

For the rest of evening, Edward didn't hear a single word Mary said to him. There was nothing particularly unusual in this, but on this occasion it wasn't the television or the crossword which occupied his mind. He was completely distracted by the concept of his new-found hair. He wasn't a particularly academic man - five O levels and a distinction in woodwork - but he read a lot of newspapers and watched documentaries and the news, and never before had he heard of baldness being anything other than a one-way process, other than with the aid of a scalpel and triangular cuttings from under the armpit.

Perhaps he was a medical phenomenon. Perhaps he could make a fortune from scientists extracting his genes and turning them into a tablet, or a spray.

From a personal point of view - even though the baldness had never consciously been a big deal - he suddenly felt his confidence lift immensely. But there was a bigger issue here, so much so that he even made the decision, totally against character, to visit his local doctor, armed with a ten-year-old Polaroid, to get a second opinion.

Doctor Patel had been in the village for over

eighteen years, and had only ever seen Edward on official business once before - for a tetanus jab following a disagreement with a garden fork. The fork had hurt slightly less than the needle, and had chosen a far more civilized point of entry, so Edward was, from that moment forward, put off the whole business of modern medicine and its practitioners, preferring in future to opt for a combination of self-diagnosis and the tactic of pushing the local chemist slowly up the rich list until he eventually retired with a yacht in St Tropez.

"Mr Jones!" beamed Dr Patel. "I haven't seen you for a long time."

Edward resisted the temptation to say "No, I've been ill" - a joke he'd admired since he was a child - and instead began silently practising his opening line while the doctor scanned his medical notes.

"Now, let me see - last time I saw you it was for…a Tetanus jab."

"Yes."

"Mmm. Well?"

"Well, that worked – I didn't get Tetanus."

Doctor Patel, who had recently undergone a fairly lengthy joke by-pass operation, slowly looked up and fixed Edward with a steely stare. "What can I do for you this time, Mr Jones?"

"Oh, right. Erm…this is going to sound silly."

"Probably. Try me."

"Take a look at this."

As Edward reached for the Polaroid from his inside jacket pocket, he felt confident that, quite apart from any professional opinion, the good doctor would be hooked on his story for purely personal reasons. After all, the last time Edward visited the surgery, Dr Patel himself had displayed a fine head of hair. Now, several million prescriptions for antibiotics later, there were no more than eight black sprigs glued together with gel. He passed the photograph over the desk and wafted it seductively in front of the doctor's eyes.

"What is it?" asked Patel flatly.

"It's a photograph," replied Edward helpfully.

"I realize that. What does it depict?"

"It's my head. The top of my head."

Doctor Patel rose wearily to his feet and briefly surveyed the top of Edward's scalp.

"So it is." He slumped back into his chair. "And?"

"Bear with me," said Edward. "What do you see, in the photograph?"

"The top of your head."

"And what don't you see?"

"Sydney Opera House. Can we get to the point?"

Edward was beginning to sense that his GP had more patients than patience, but he persevered.

"All right - now take a look at this one."

Edward produced a second, more crumpled Polaroid, and thrust it theatrically in front of the doctor's face.

"A fuzzy picture of the moon," said Patel, who was becoming more frosty by the second.

"It's my head again. That...is a bald patch." Edward's delivery of the punchline was almost cheesy enough to merit being accompanied by a knowing wink. The doctor started chewing on his bottom lip.

"So?"

"So, that picture was taken ten years ago. We'd just had some new mirror wardrobes fitted and I accidentally caught sight of myself, through a hand mirror, from behind. I hadn't noticed it before."

The good doctor could now legitimately be described as tetchy, if not just plain snappy. "Why are you here, Mr Jones?"

Edward, feeling the heat of the doctor's stern mental examination, dispensed with the niceties of punctuation and started gabbling furiously. Patel used the time wisely to ignore him and catch up with his paperwork.

"The bald patch - it was a bit of a shock, to be honest - it upset me...I ended up taking a picture of it, with my Polaroid, and I got very depressed for a while and then I decided...well, not to look any more...what you don't see can't hurt you, sort of thing, and that's how it's been, well, until last Friday night - it was my birthday..."

"Many happy returns…"

"…thank you, and something - I don't know what - well, I just had this urge to have another peek, just to see how bad it was because I was expecting, you know, like a saucer or something, so, when I saw…well, that, I was sort of shocked, really, in a sort of pleasant way…so, what do you think?"

Patel checked himself for a moment, to make sure that Edward had now finally reached the end of his epic sentence.

"What do I think about what?"

"All of it."

The doctor exhaled like a steam hammer, sank his head back into his old leather chair, and screwed his eyes tightly shut.

"Mr Jones, I've got patients waiting out there with illnesses."

"I might be ill."

"I don't think so."

"But my hair…"

"Hair is not life-threatening, Mr Jones."

"But…don't you think I should have my head examined?"

The doctor's eyes narrowed down to a venomous slit. "Don't tempt me, Mr Jones."

"Aren't you at least going to take a look?"

Patel slammed down his pen, slid his chair back on its castors, opened a desk drawer, and plucked out a pair of surgical gloves. With all the enthusiasm of a man about to perform a rectal examination on a constipated bull elephant, he stretched, slapped and twanged the rubber sheaths unceremoniously onto his waggling fingers and started brusquely poking at Edward's scalp, as if he were looking for nits.

He studied the Polaroid, frowned, and studied the scalp again. This was clearly outside of his normal territory, so he resorted to more familiar tactics, prodding around with a stethoscope - at one point bizarrely placing it on Edward's scalp and asking him to breathe in - and then he tested his blood pressure. But Edward sensed this all had more to do with playing for time than with any real diagnosis.

After five minutes of grumpy silence and some distinctly dubious medical practice, Dr Patel tugged the surgical gloves from his hands and discarded them resentfully in the bin, a gesture clearly designed to make the patient feel he'd wasted another 30p of NHS money. Finally, the medicine man spoke.

"There's nothing wrong with you."

"But…what about the hair?"

"These things can happen, Mr Jones. Sometimes women lose their hair temporarily when they have psoriasis, but it grows back."

"I'm not a woman, and I haven't got psoriasis."

Edward hadn't spent seven years at medical school, but he felt on solid ground with both points.

"Just be grateful!" hissed the exasperated doctor, finally raising his voice in anger. "Look at me. I used to have hair. Then I became a doctor. Then I had patients like you!"

This seemed a bit harsh. Edward didn't respond - he just sulked like a scolded schoolboy, and quietly began gathering his photographs. Patel calmed down, softened his tone and tried again. "Mr Jones, please. You're a healthy man. Enjoy it."

Edward fussily tapped his precious Polaroids into perfect alignment on Patel's desk and slipped them back into his pocket. "So that's it, then, is it?"

"I'm a doctor. If you're worried about having too much hair, I suggest you visit your hairdresser."

He came in search of trained medical opinion. Sarcasm he could do without. Edward's reponse was instinctive. "Do you think I should see a specialist?

That was it. Edward saw the doctor stiffen. For "Do you think I should see a specialist?" read "You're out of your depth, pal - move over and let a real doctor have a look." Dr Patel cut short the interview, offering the parting shot that Edward's tetanus jab could do with a booster. Edward knew where the tetanus jab was destined, and it was clear that revenge was on the doctor's mind, so he left while he still had his trousers on. But the incident just made him even more determined to get to the bottom of things, if that's the phrase I want. In fact, a strange sort of stubborn, confident, obsessive determination was creeping up on him. He was a new Edward. The old Edward would have just let this drop. The old Edward wouldn't even have picked it up in the first place. The new one simply redoubled his efforts. He suddenly remembered Mr Rogers, the stick insect consultant with the caterpillar eyebrows. He had only seen him twice, and that was five years ago - the caterpillars were probably butterflies by now - but there was something about his face which inspired hope. It was a charismatic, kind, knowledgeable face. Edward made up his mind to find him and to involve him in his strange quest for the truth.

With the new Edward very much in the driving seat, he found his van steering mysteriously away from the damaged pylon designated on his worksheet, and towards the Shropshire hospital which had taken possession of his charred remains some five years earlier. The hospital receptionist eyed Edward cautiously.

"Mr Rogers, you say?"

She had the sort of voice that instantly made you want to slap her. Even though she'd only said four words, they took over a minute each to emerge, because she spoke with a dense Black Country drawl so outrageously dozy that it left you thinking that she must spend her tea breaks sniffing the anaesthetist's tanks.

"Yes," replied Edward when his turn eventually

came. "He's a consultant here. Very tall man. Thin. Eyebrows."

"And have you got an appointment with Mr Rogers?" she spent the next ten minutes asking.

"Erm, no…not exactly. I'd just like to talk to him for a moment."

"Thank goodness. Mr Rogers retired last year."

"Oh."

"But you wouldn't be the first to turn up for an appointment with him. That's the NHS for you - long waiting list, crap system. The I.T. people have been promising to sort it out since last April, but it never happens. I've had three people after Mr Rogers this month already. And one woman came for her appointment with Mr Akerson, and he's been dead six years."

Edward wondered how many others had died just waiting for her to finish talking. He tried to inject some urgency and purpose into the situation. "Right, well, can you tell me how I could get in touch with him?"

"Mr Akerson?"

"Mr Rogers."

"Not allowed to give out addresses I'm afraid. Against hospital rules. Mr Akerson's a different matter, though. My sister Julie's a well-respected clairvoyant, and…"

"But you could contact him - Mr Rogers?"

"In theory."

What the hell did that mean? 'In theory.' Could she or couldn't she? What sort of utter nebulous bollocks is 'In theory'? He wasn't asking for an opinion on how the universe started - just a quick phone call. And how could two words take up most of his afternoon? Edward felt something snap inside.

"Right, then - put the theory into practice. Here's my number...and my name...please call Mr Rogers and tell him to get in touch with me as soon as possible. Tell him it's important. Tell him I'm the one who got struck by lightning - black face, one eyebrow, raccoon eyes, five years ago. Got it? Don't answer, just nod. Good. Thank you for your time."

And with that, Edward marched out of the hospital. For a while, he just sat on the steps outside, his head spinning. Where the hell had this dominant alter-ego come from? For the first time in his life, he found himself saying the things he used to only think. The man who wouldn't say 'boo' to a goose had suddenly acquired a taste for pate de fois gras.

It was Friday. It was ham. And Edward was up a pylon when his mobile rang. It was Mr Rogers. Edward recognized those cultured tones instantly, and he felt his heart give a little thump of excitement.

"It's good of you to ring me," he heard himself

saying. "I know you're retired, but I have a condition which I think might interest you from an intellectual point of view. I believe it's totally unique - and potentially hugely significant, both medically and financially - but my own doctor is under-qualified and far too short-sighted to realize its importance. I'm not prepared to say any more over the phone. I'd like us to meet and discuss it face-to-face. Have you any time this week - later today perhaps, around four?"

The old Edward gasped in admiration at the new Edward. He was magnificent. Polite, but clinically to the point, and devastatingly authoritative. In this mood, Edward could sell timeshares to gypsies, or pvc windows to Prince Charles. He could persuade three-quarters of England to switch to a more expensive electricity provider. He could extract huge charitable donations from the heads of multinationals. He could convince the American President to sign up to reduced carbon emissions, inspire Bob Geldof to write decent songs, and get production companies to stop making reality TV shows. He could do anything he wanted to.

Somewhere on the other end of the line, an exotic pair of caterpillars rose in unison. Mr Rogers, now merely a retired figure of authority, gave way to the new kid on the block. He was putty in Edward's hands, and instantly offered his address.

An appointment was made for four o'clock that afternoon. The pylon with the dodgy connector would have to wait.

CHAPTER FOUR

A neatly trimmed pair of topiary peacocks greeted Edward as he walked up the gravel driveway of Mr Rogers' elegant country retreat. Edward wondered whether Rogers, in the boredom of retirement, had been tempted to perform similar miracles with his eyebrows, inventing a new sort of human bonsai topiary. He easily had enough raw material to start work on a couple of superb peacocks, and he felt sure that once the job was completed the National Trust would step in with an offer to maintain them.

As the door opened, though, it was clear that Rogers had preferred to let nature take its course. And what a course.

One eyebrow, the one occupying the left half of the doorway, had been extended considerably, and now had its own spiral staircase to an upper floor. Rococo squiggles decorated the outer perimeters, and there was sisal carpeting throughout. The other eyebrow, not to be outdone, had taken its original role of keeping sweat out of the eyes to a whole new level, and now provided a thatched canopy capable of keeping Mr Rogers' shoes dry. And somewhere behind all of this lay Mr Rogers himself.

Five years on, and out of the context of the hospital setting, he looked far frailer than Edward had remembered. He was still ridiculously tall, but this was tempered by a slight stoop reminiscent of a Lowry figure, and there was a vulnerability about him which instantly tinged Edward with sadness. That face, all that knowledge, at the mercy of such a fragile frame.

"Mr Jones, I presume?" The voice, at least, had lost none of its impressive sonority.

Edward confirmed that it was, and he was duly invited in.

"Sorry, I don't remember the face. I thought I might. One of the side-effects of old age, I'm afraid. Do you know how many brain cells we lose every day, Mr Jones?"

Edward confessed that he didn't.

"You'd be amazed. Erm…I can't seem to recall the exact figure myself any more. But it is a lot. Sit down, please. Would you like my wife to bring us some tea?"

Edward wasn't quite sure how to answer this. If it meant would he like tea, then possibly. If it meant would he like his wife to bring it, as opposed to someone else, well…

"No, thanks. I'm fine. I'm not going to take up any more of your time than necessary, I just wanted an intelligent medical opinion on something that's happened to me. I think it's significant, but you might tell me it happens all the time and make me feel a complete fool. Either way, I'll trust your opinion. It all started, well...take a look at this photograph."

Edward handed over the bent and faded Polaroid. Mr Rogers took a while to find focus, bringing it first close to his face, then away at arm's length, then taking it to the window for extra light, until he finally realized the image itself was not in focus.

"Ah! The moon."

"My head. A bald patch."

"Oh. Yes. Yes, I see it now."

"That was taken ten years ago, when I was thirty-five. Take a look at my head now."

A slightly wary Mr Rogers circled round to view Edward's head.

"Would you mind coming by the window, only my eyes..."

Edward dutifully crouched down by the large, opened leaded window, and Mr Rogers began warming to his task.

"Would you mind if I...ruffled you up a bit?"

"Ruffle away," said Edward, clearly thrilled that someone was at last taking it seriously.

The ensuing examination was indeed impressively thorough. At one point, Mr Rogers went to a bureau and produced a large magnifying glass. Now this was a real doctor, thought Edward. At last, the oracle spoke.

"You seem to have re-grown most of your hair."

"Yes."

"The photograph – it is definitely you, I presume?"

Edward confirmed that there were no other heads in the vicinity when he took the photograph.

"And you haven't taken any special medication over the last few years?"

"A few Lem Sips. Nothing else."

"Mmm."

The doctor leaned forward with the magnifying glass for one last telling close-up by the window. Perfect timing, as the summer sun suddenly cut through a gap in the clouds, flooded the lens with pure energy, and singed a tiny laser beam dot into Edward's scalp.

"Arrgh!" Edward went to ground like he'd been hit by a sniper.

"Oh, I'm sorry. I'm so sorry!" gushed a red-faced Rogers. "Are you all right?"

Edward got up, warily stroking the carpet pile from his knees, checking that he hadn't once again been the victim of a sneaky doctor's syringe.

"Do forgive me," pleaded Rogers again. "Haven't

done that in years. Used to set fire to leaves when I was a child. Amazing phenomenon, though, don't you think?"

Edward's enthusiasm for the impromptu physics lesson was, at best, muted. He was beginning to think that he had somehow offended Nature, and it was out to punish him with a series of short, sharp shocks. Rattled by forked lightning on a summer's afternoon. Severely sunburnt - whilst indoors - in less than a second. All he needed now was to jump into bed with a wayward box jelly-fish and he'd have the set.

"Are you sure you won't have some tea?" Rogers enquired again, desperate to make amends.

"No, thank you. I've taken up enough of your time," replied Edward, nervously scanning the carpet for pet scorpions. "So, what's the verdict - about the hair?"

"Mr Jones, I also have a Polaroid camera - would you mind?"

"Help yourself."

The stick insect doctor scurried off into an adjoining room. Polaroid cameras run on batteries, reasoned Edward. The chance of being wounded by one was remote. But then again, the chances of being struck by…

Rogers was back, proudly clutching his camera.

"Would you mind crouching down? That's it. Lower. Just a little lower. Perfect. Stay exactly as you are, please."

The genial doctor was taking great care to get exactly the same angle as the original photograph. Edward knew he'd come to the right man. But he was wrong about the chances of being wounded by a Polaroid camera. They are, of course, considerably larger than conventional cameras, and while having one dropped directly onto your skull from two and a half feet is never perhaps going to be life-threatening, it's certainly no picnic.

Mr Rogers couldn't apologize enough to the bewildered and prostrate Edward. The doctor's arthritic fingers, struggling to find the ideal camera position, had momentarily lost their grip on the casing, and it was only then that Edward realized just how painful arthritis can be. It was becoming increasingly clear why retirement had been the sensible option for this once fine surgeon. He still possessed a wonderful wealth of knowledge and marvellous bedside manner, but in the last few years he had developed an accident-prone nature which earned him the nickname of "Doctor Clouseau" amongst his colleagues.

The final straw had come when three junior surgeons and an anaesthetist had to give chase on hands and knees after a replacement liver had squirted from Mr Rogers' hands, like a lively trout making a desperate bid for freedom. Okay, so the liver was eventually caught, swilled off and plumbed in without further incident, and the recipient lived to be blissfully ignorant of the cover-up. But Mr Rogers' confidence had taken a big hit. He knew it was time to hang up his scalpel.

Edward, of course, knew none of this. Indeed, it was a few moments before he knew anything at all. Certain remote tribes refuse to be photographed, believing it robs them of their soul. Edward was now firmly in their camp, and it took all of Mr Rogers' considerable charm to persuade Edward to let him to have another crack at it.

Eventually, though, the shot was taken. But only after Edward had carefully masked off all the superfluous parts of his head with pillows. The doctor looked very pleased with the results, and carefully signed and dated the new evidence, in ink, on the back.

"The date's important you see because, well, look here. See? It looks to all intents and purposes like a typical case of male pattern baldness, before and after. But it's in reverse. The before should be the after, and the after the before. Fascinating. I'd like to show these to a friend of mine - Jack Nugent. He's a trichologist."

Excellent. He'd been recommended to a circus act.

"He'll probably want to examine you himself, if that's all right?"

Edward wasn't sure if he could survive another examination without investing in a motorcycle helmet, but nodded appreciatively. Rogers was a good man. A tad clumsy, perhaps, and a few years past the surgeon's equivalent of a sell-by date, but good.

As Edward said his goodbyes and strolled back up the gravel path to his van, more subtle evidence of Rogers' unfortunate demise confronted him. He hadn't noticed it before, but one of the topiary peacocks was missing its head.

A momentary slip with the clippers, no doubt. A lifetime of cultivation blighted in an instant by a frustrating combination of uncertain hands and failing eyesight.

"Sad," he reflected. "But I suppose old age comes to us all."

It would be another two weeks before he realized the extraordinary irony of what he'd just said.

CHAPTER FIVE

Edward's appointment with Jack Nugent came astonishingly quickly. It came by telephone, and it came within twenty-four hours. Edward's condition had clearly caught the imagination of his elderly confidant, and Rogers had wasted no time in contacting his trichologist colleague.

Edward's mobile went just as he was tucking into a ham sandwich. It was Friday.

"Mr Jenkins?"

"Jones."

"Oh, sorry. I was told Jenkins. My name's Ted Nugent. I'm a doctor. Mr Rogers asked me to get in touch."

"Oh. Right. I was expecting you. Only not so soon. And he said your name was Jack."

"Yes, right. I'm afraid Peter's memory is getting a little slippy these days, bless him. He called me John when he rang. But I am Ted. Edward, actually. And you are?"

"Edward."

"Oh, right. Easy enough then."

Formal introductions now concluded, Ted Nugent made an appointment for Edward to see him three days later at the hospital. Three days? Take out the weekend and we're basically talking next day. Does that sound like the NHS to you? Edward was rather intrigued to see how much he was being fast-tracked through the system. No two-year waiting list for him. Had he urgently needed a new hip, or replacement heart valve, he would no doubt have languished at the end of an elastic queue. But here he was, offering the merest whiff of a condition which could add value to a consultant's reputation or bank account, and he was being hurriedly strapped into an NHS rocket ship bound for the top man.

Edward tried to alleviate a slight guilty feeling by reasoning that a consultation with a hair specialist was unlikely to push another, needier patient further down the line. After all, hair was hair, and hips were hips. The worst that could happen was that he'd defer a balding man's appointment with destiny. And who knows - he might even turn out to be that bald man's salvation, by being the catalyst for a new miracle cure.

He wasn't, however, expecting to meet that bald man quite so soon.

Ted Nugent, consultant trichologist, was that bald man. He was completely bald. Outrageously bald.

Cartoon bald.

Now, a completely bald hair specialist is, when you scratch below the surface, just the sort of bloke you want on your side. After all, he understands the problem. He's driven by the right sort of emotions. Think of him not as an independent adviser, but as a genuine grass-roots shareholder - someone who owns a slice of the action - and suddenly his chosen career seems both obvious and inspired. But, despite all that, somehow the initial visual impact is, well, disappointing.

So it was a slightly deflated Edward that shook the hand of the overweight, dishevelled, sweaty, bald, blunt-speaking Yorkshireman that was Mr Nugent.

"Edward!"

"Mr Nugent?"

"Disappointed?"

"Er…no, I…"

"Let me guess. You were expecting your hair specialist to have hair."

"Well…"

"I know, I know…it's like having an appointment with an ugly beauty therapist, or a fat keep-fit instructor. It shouldn't reflect on their ability to teach the subject, but it does. Deep down you're thinking, if he's so damn good, why does he still look like a snooker ball?"

"I'm not questioning your…"

"It's human nature, Edward. People want their beauty therapist to be beautiful, their keep-fit instructor to be fit, in the same way that you want your hair specialist to be hairy. As a totem. A sign of hope."

"Look, I…"

"Let me tell you something, Edward Jones. You'll soon learn that modesty is not amongst my long list of qualities. As a young man in the world of science and medicine I was seriously hot news. I could have been anything I wanted. And then…this happened."

Nugent prodded his finger aggressively into the top of his scalp. "This, Edward, is the reason I do what I do."

"Okay, okay. Qualifications accepted."

Edward, now pinned against the desk, offered the uneasy, frozen grin of a man trapped in a lift with a psychopath. Nugent emerged from a private trance and, perhaps sensing he may have gone in a little too heavy for a first appointment, offered Edward a faint, withered smile. "Not that you have my problem."

"No," squeaked Edward, "more the opposite really." And as soon as he'd said it, he wished he hadn't - uncertain whether Nugent would suddenly turn on him and begin another wild-eyed rant. But he didn't. He switched with schizophrenic ease into the world's most charming and welcoming doctor.

"And that is what intrigues me. May I?"

"Er…help yourself."

Nugent leaned forward, peered for a split second at Edward's crown, and then, without even lifting a finger to touch him, he slumped back down behind his desk and started tapping numbers into a laptop.

Edward was nonplussed. "Is that it?"

"What - disappointed in me again?"

Edward didn't want to push his luck, but thought he had to defend his corner. "Well, I did think…"

"No."

Nugent stopped Edward dead with a look. An extraordinary look. In an instant, he'd switched persona again. From dishevelled bald man, to psychopath, to genial doctor, to man of steel. His eyes fixed on Edward like tractor beams. "No, I haven't finished with you yet, Edward. There's a screen back there. Strip to the underpants."

You didn't argue with a stare like that. Edward silently reversed behind the screen and did as he was told.

From an unpromising start, Edward was soon won over. Nugent, in short, was magnificent. No quick check of the scalp under a bright light for this man - oh, no. Blood pressure, weight, saliva, urine and blood samples, armpit swabs, lung capacity, ear nose and throat exploration, nail cuttings, chest and pubic hair cuttings, foot scrapings, retina scans - everything which could legally be done to a living body in the pursuit of science was done at least once, sometimes twice for luck, not to mention a rigorous mental examination which felt like an hour in the Mastermind chair - specialist subject, the innermost thoughts and feelings of Edward Jones.

As Edward buttoned up his shirt three hours later, he felt like his entire being - mind, body and soul - had been nibbled into small pieces and taken away for analysis by a huge army of professor ants. He'd clearly misjudged Nugent. The earlier erratic outbursts of aggression were merely the symptoms of Nugent's intensity. Here was a deeply thoughtful and dedicated man, but one who was also plagued with the occasional dark and unfathomable moods that accompany true genius.

"Well, Edward," announced Nugent finally, "I think we've made a good start."

"Start?"

"I shall have to do all this again, I'm afraid, in a week's time. Comparative data, you see."

Edward wasn't sure that he did see. But he duly attended another intensive session, seven days later, just as rigorous as the last.

"Fascinating," declared Nugent, as he held a test tube full of Edward's juices up to the light. He gave it a good shake, squinted deep into the settling sediment, and scribbled some hieroglyphics onto a notepad. "Right. That should be all I need. I'll be in touch in a week or so."

He then did something which Edward thought totally out of character. He patted him gently on the shoulder.

"Don't worry."

Edward frowned. "Should I be worried?"

"Erm…no."

"Now I'm worried."

"Don't be. I'll get to the bottom of it."

Nugent shook the hand of his exhausted, impressed and now slightly worried guinea pig. The door closed abruptly, but through its small glass panel Edward caught sight of Nugent rushing straight back to his desk, where he'd already begun examining a pulsating mass of graphical data flashing on the screen of his laptop. Wow. This was one excited scientist.

Edward decided to take the rest of the day off. He didn't go home, just for a walk around some nearby parkland. He wanted some air, some space, some quality thinking time. He hadn't confided in Mary since this whole business began. She wouldn't understand, he reasoned. She rarely understood. He'd always kept it simple with Mary - talking about ham sandwiches, tie-clips, Martin, Aunty Joan, shopping and reality TV, but never about politics, sex, emotions, himself, herself, or the future. It seemed to work, in a numb, disconnected sort of way. It worked in the sense that there were no blinding rows between them.

Edward returned home at his normal time, and sank down into his customary seat.

"How was your day?" said Mary automatically, not even looking up.

"All right."

"Mend any pylons?"

"A few."

"Good."

Their long chat over, Mary returned to the hypnotic spell of the television and the comfort of her box of chocolates. Edward glanced over at Mary as she sat on her separate sofa. What he saw disturbed him. He hadn't really noticed it before - perhaps he just hadn't looked. But there was no denying it. In the last few years, Mary's face had imperceptibly morphed from youthful middle age to early old age. His wife had become Aunty Joan.

Edward jumped up and made his way to the bathroom. He stood for a full minute in front of the mirror, completely in the dark. He knew it was a minute, because he silently counted down the seconds, though he didn't quite know why. As he reached zero, he took a deep breath, reached out with his left hand, and tugged on the light cord.

No. Not him. Not yet. Thank God.

Not even allowing for a generous portion of bias, Edward was convinced that he was not staring at an old man in the making. This was, surely, by any objective measure, still a relatively youthful countenance. His wife may be Aunty Joan, but he had not yet become Uncle Peter and, for that at least, he quietly gave thanks.

In fact, with all the excitement of his recent visit to Nugent, and the confidence boost he'd received by renewing his acquaintance with some long-forsaken follicles, Edward was generally feeling quite energized of late. He had a spring in his step and a sharpness in his thinking which he hadn't felt for years. He'd long since forgotten about Nugent's request not to worry, which traditionally would have been a major cause for concern, and seemed to have a generally positive outlook about, well, most things. It was very welcome, but very odd, and not very Edward. Some mornings he was only a heartbeat away from singing in the shower. Smiling was surely just around the corner. If these were the early rumblings of his mid-life crisis, bring it on.

*   *   *

The working week melted away, and it seemed like no time at all before Edward was once again enjoying the familiar delights of a high-altitude ham sandwich. He had a unique vantage point, dangling at the summit of one of the main-line pylons which straddled the Gloucestershire countryside like a series of cut and paste Eiffel Towers, and he could see for miles.

Now there was another curious thing. Seeing for miles. And yet he hadn't bothered with his glasses for months.

Edward first realized it was time to visit the optician when he was thirty-six. Yes, exactly thirty-six, he remembered, because that was when Mary had pointed out to him that he was holding all his birthday cards at arm's length, and still craning his neck backwards, in order to work out who they were from. Edward did what any self-respecting man would do in the circumstances, he completely ignored the problem and hoped it would go away. But by his thirty-seventh birthday, it was clear that not only had it not gone away, it had degenerated apace. No longer was it sufficient to hold the cards at arm's length to get a crisp image. He was now obliged to prop them up on the mantelpiece and step backwards into the garden. By the time he'd finally got the writing in focus, it was too far away to read.

A quick check-up revealed that his left eye was letting the side down badly, and was probably also responsible for a recent spate of headaches. So Edward decided to save the twenty pounds a week he was spending on painkillers and re-invest it in eye-care. To be fair, the eye test revealed that Edward only needed glasses for detailed close-up work, such as finding his car, recognizing his wife, and not bumping into doors, but it was a major blow to his pride to realize that, from that moment forth, he would forever be reliant on artificial aids. It was a slippery slope. Okay, he was still at the top of it, but that's the problem with slippery slopes, you don't stay there for long.

He emerged from the optician looking like a cross between Nana Mouskouri and Elvis Costello. He hated seeing himself in the mirror, and the irony was that he now could. But at least the headaches stopped, and he could suddenly read things without having to have arms like a gibbon, so there were upsides.

One day, however, about three months ago, he'd accidentally trodden on his spectacles (he didn't see them) but nevertheless decided to gamely press on with his usual lunchtime pylon diversion of trying to tackle the Daily Mail crossword. To his amazement, he found he could not only see the newspaper, but also read it, and he could do this without having to place it down on the ground while he remained up the pylon. The technique of hoping the problem would just go away seemed to have finally borne fruit. At £120 a pair, he wasn't in a particular rush to replace the specs, and had therefore lived quite happily without them ever since.

The crossword was completed in record time. Thirteen across was a bit of a stinker - Capital of Albania - but Edward managed to pluck the answer from his memory banks with consummate ease. Tirane. Very satisfying.

There was a time when he was getting a bit worried about his memory. Short-term memory loss is one of the more insidious side-effects of getting older, along with long-term memory loss and medium-term memory loss, and Edward had in recent years become acutely aware that he was not immune. Words, names, facts and places that he used to slide into sentences without even thinking were occasionally being replaced by 'erms'.

Erms, of course, are fine in short measure. They are the sound the mouth makes to keep the listener entertained while the brain is desperately rifling through the grey filing cabinet for the correct information. They're a bit like the egg timer on a computer with insufficient RAM. The trouble is, brains are not as easy as computers to upgrade, and when you find there are more erms than words, it can get rather tedious for both parties.

Occasionally, on a bad day, a brain will even mislay the word erm, and replace it with a strange lifeless pause, where the eyes lose their glint, giving the effect that someone has momentarily become detached from their power supply.

Edward had experienced a few of those moments, and they were always a little disturbing. He might have worried about them more, if he'd remembered to. On one occasion he introduced his wife to a colleague in the street, and there was a definite four second dead spot between saying "my wife…", and successfully locating her name "erm…Mary." At the time he'd laughed it off, saying he was distracted by a pigeon, but the incident, unlike his wife's name, had stuck in his mind.

Just lately, though, Edward had to admit that his

brain had started to feel considerably sharper. He put it down to the fact that he was drinking more water.

In a bored moment at the breakfast table, he'd recently read on the back of a bottle that drinking copious amounts of water, amongst its many other health benefits, also helps with your concentration. 'Up to 30% improvement' it had boldly claimed. That, unless he wasn't concentrating properly, was nearly one-third, quite an astonishing statistic. So, on a trial period, he began substituting his tea habit with a water habit. It seemed to have worked.

What they failed to mention on the bottle, of course, was one of the major downsides of de-toxing in this way. You need to have a bladder with the capacity of Loch Ness. Having to have a wee every twelve minutes can be inconvenient at the best of times, but if you spend half your working day sixty feet up an electricity pylon, it tends to pose logistical problems that can only be solved by grandiose exhibitionism.

A cautionary tale for anyone with a convertible vehicle.

As Edward zipped up his flies and watched the long, frustrated snake of Friday afternoon traffic slowly wriggle its way along the motorway, his mobile rang. But he didn't answer it. Why should he? He didn't hear it. He'd left his mobile in the van, sixty feet below.

And thus it was that, while an unsuspecting

maintenance man nonchalantly watched the world go by from the comfort of his Gloucestershire pylon, seventy miles away an anxious doctor was taking a deep breath, steadying his nerve, and preparing to leave the world's most extraordinary voice-mail.

CHAPTER SIX

When it came to the crunch, he just couldn't do it.

How can you possibly explain to someone the full significance of what he, Doctor Edward Nugent, had discovered, on the voice-mail of a mobile phone? After all, this wasn't just significant, it was mind-blowingly, earth-shatteringly significant. It could fill every back issue of the medical journals since time began and still be next week's sell-out exclusive. It could have its own show on the BBC - no, its own digital channel - every night, twenty-four hours a day, and still the licence payers would clamour for more. It would spawn opinion, research, chat rooms, uploads and downloads sufficient to seize up the worldwide web. It would send the paparazzi into an uncontrollable feeding frenzy. Spin doctors could only underplay it. In short, it was big deal.

So, no matter how eloquently Ted Nugent had tried to summarize the facts, he couldn't hope to fit them onto a sixty second voice-mail and expect to do them justice.

There was a moment, a brief moment, where he felt the need to blurt out his findings like an excited schoolboy but, when it came to the crunch, and the electronic lady asked him to speak clearly after the tone, there was a gulp and a long, brittle pause.

"Edward? Ted Nugent. Erm...can you call me back?"

"To listen to the message again, press one. To save the message, press two. To delete the message, press three."

Edward pressed one. The content of the message was clear enough, but he felt distinctly uneasy about its tone. He listened again, and again, and then a fourth time, but it didn't help. Nugent definitely sounded anxious. Like a man with bad news to impart. But this was no ordinary bearer of bad news - this was a doctor. Let's face it, on the "I've got some bad news for you" Richter scale, doctors hit a maximum ten every time - altogether a different league from the mild tremors caused by your accountant, or the man doing your MOT.

All sorts of uneasy thoughts whirred through Edward's mind. Had Nugent found some dread disease? Is there such a thing as hair cancer? You can tell anything from blood tests these days, especially when they're backed up with urine, saliva and DNA sampling. Perhaps he'd only got weeks to live. Days. Hours. But he'd been feeling fine. Better than ever. So it was with a pounding heart that Edward finally hit the hash key on his mobile to return Nugent's call. It was six-forty on a

Friday evening. Chances are, the good doctor was now settled in front of his log fire with his pipe and slippers, and Edward suddenly realized that he may have to face the unbearable agony of not knowing his fate until Monday morning. That's if he lived until Monday morning. Perhaps he had some obscure teutonic-sounding medical syndrome which meant he'd be whistling one minute and drop like a pole-axed bull the next. Shit! Damn it! Why the hell did he forget to take his mobile up the pylon? If only he'd….

He needn't have worried. At least about the pipe and slippers. The phone on the other end managed just half a ring before Nugent pounced to answer it. But that in itself, of course, did nothing to calm Edward's building sense of doom. As he heard the doctor's voice, all the moisture in his mouth suddenly took a holiday.

"Edward?"

"Yes."

"Thanks for ringing back. Erm…I've completed the tests."

"Yes."

"Look, I'll get straight to the point."

"Yes."

"Can you come and see me, Monday morning?"

"Yes."

"Good. Nine o'clock?"

"Yes."

"Can't really explain over the phone, but erm... well, interesting stuff. See you Monday, yes?"

"Yes."

"Goodnight."

"Yes."

And he was gone.

Edward sat on the side of the road in his van, staring at his mobile as if it had just betrayed him. The most important conversation of his life, and all he could manage was one word. "Yes."

Terrific. He could have performed his part in the dialogue just as well at eighteen months old. Indeed, he could have chosen to conduct the whole conversation in French, Spanish, German, Italian, Russian - or even, thanks to the intelligence gained from a recent Daily Mail crossword answer, Swahili - and still managed it comfortably. Why hadn't he demanded there and then to know what Nugent had found? Why hadn't he cross-examined him in microscopic detail? What had happened to the new assertive Edward Jones? His heart was bouncing like a basketball in an exhibition match. A horrible irony was at work - he'd been feeling so good lately, so positive, that the thought of it all coming crashing down suddenly had the power to affect him more than it ever could have done before. Now, he was enjoying life. So now he had more to lose.

"Hold on to the positives, Edward," he muttered to himself. "Don't get carried away. He said he'll see me on Monday. So that means I'll still be alive on Monday. But maybe not on Tuesday. But surely he would have told me if I was d…but on the other hand…"

Too many buts. He couldn't stand it any longer. He was ringing Nugent back. He didn't want to, but his thumbs weren't giving him a choice - they were already dialing the number. Personally, he was quite happy to wait until Monday, but his thumbs obviously needed to know the facts right now.

Bugger, bugger, bugger. This time it was ringing out. How could it? Only twenty seconds earlier Nugent had pounced like a farmer's cat on a field mouse to answer that phone. Now what? Doesn't he realize it's me again? Or perhaps he *does* realize it's me again. Perhaps that's just it. Perhaps he's just staring at the handset, scared to pick it up. Or perhaps he's in the toilet. Yes, that could be it. Even doctors have to go to the toilet. Let it ring. Come on, damn it, answer. Shit! Voice mail. Do I leave a message? Do I ask him if he's in the toilet? Do I ask him if he's gone home? Do I ask him if I'm going to die?

There was a long, brittle pause. "Dr Nugent, it's Edward Jones. Erm…can you call me back?"

But Nugent didn't. He was on his way home to his pipe and slippers. And it was the longest weekend of Edward's life.

CHAPTER SEVEN

Nine o'clock on Monday morning, as agreed, Edward Jones was waiting outside Nugent's office. Actually, Edward was a tad early. It was six-fifteen. But you couldn't blame an anxious man for being a little impatient. He hadn't slept, shaved or eaten since Friday, and he was beginning to look worthy of the prognosis that he'd imagined Nugent was about to pronounce on him.

Nugent was also early. He arrived at five to nine, and looked a little flustered to see that Edward was already there, slumped in his doorway like a destitute.

"My God, you look dreadful" was the doctor's opening gambit - the perfect way to settle Edward's nerves. "You'd better come in."

As they entered his office, Nugent gathered by the way that Edward slammed the door, pinned him to the wall, and clasped his cheeks firmly in both hands to ensure unfailing eye contact, that perhaps something was on his mind.

"I need to know. Now. Please."

"Okay. Okay. I'm soggy," said Nugent, his voice cruelly distorted through two squashed cheeks. Edward slowly released his grip, but his stare continued to hold the doctor in a vice-like grip.

"You're soggy?"

"I didn't realize I'd got you so worried. Sit down."

Oops. Nugent had said the wrong thing again. Asking someone to sit down is a traditional precursor to bad news, and it didn't escape Edward's notice. What little blood was still resident in his face squirted instantly down to his toes, leaving him on the teetering edge of consciousness.

"No, not sit down. Anything but sit down. I'm going to die, aren't I?"

"Edward, it's not like that, it's…it's…well, it's different. Look, will you please sit down?"

Edward did even better than that. He passed out. There was a momentary buzzing noise, a blue wash came across his eyes, and over he went, without waiting for permission to land. But this was no unspectacular slump to the ground. It was a magnificent aerial display. Edward's stiffened body, elegantly and without fuss, rotated from 0 to 90 degrees like the sweep-hand of an analogue stopwatch. He would have made it to 91 degrees, had it not been for the intervention of a hard linoleum floor, which temporarily sent him back 10 degrees north. There was a moment or two of vacillation, until gravity finally took charge. All that was missing was the shout of "Timber!" Had he been conscious, it probably would have hurt.

"Waaaa....Ed...rrrd...Edww...ight...war...right ... dward? Edward? Are you all right?"

Edward's eyelids slowly parted. Foreground, and out of focus, was some kind of huge pink blob. Beyond that floated a face with at least six dimensions. Or was it two faces with three each? Either way, it spoke in stereo. Gradually, the two images consolidated into one, the stereo panned into intelligible mono. It was Nugent. Of course it was Nugent. Who else would it be? But what was that huge pink blob? An exploratory prod with a finger explained all. It was Edward's nose. It had taken the brunt of his rapid descent to the floor, and the resultant impact had caused it to instantly swell to the size of a small dinghy.

Now, a brief word about noses. Let's be honest - noses, on the whole, are not great when it comes to a crisis. Whereas a fractured collar bone or rib, no matter how much pain it's in, will always try to struggle along with minimal fuss - even to the extent of hiding the problem from concerned by-standers - noses tend to show their feelings far too easily. They're always the first to complain when they're suffering - whether it's from a compound fracture, a zit or a common cold - and they always seem to demand to be centre of attention. Edward's nose was no different. It had announced to the world that it was gravely injured by expanding to five times its original size. And it wasn't done yet.

The only reason it wasn't pumping blood was that blood, on the whole, needs a few moments' notice to get organized, and the speed of the incident had caught it out. But within a couple of minutes of getting the red alert, Edward's beak started producing the stuff by the bucket-load.

Nugent, despite years of medical training, went into a mild state of panic, followed almost immediately by a major state of panic. Injured bodies, you see, weren't his forte. True, he was a doctor, but he'd always been into the research end of the market - cutting-edge science rather than cutting edge scalpel, as it were. Microscopes, petri dishes and computer modelling were the natural tools of his trade. The more hands-on, muck and bullets paramedic stuff had never appealed to him, and the sight of blood in particular had always been a problem.

Seeing Edward's shirt and trousers awash with a tidal wave from the Red Sea had an instant destabilizing effect on Nugent's equilibrium. In short, he too passed out. Not to be outdone by Edward's earlier impersonation of a felled Giant Redwood, the good doctor put in a superb effort of his own, easily deserving a maximum ten from the trio of Olympic judges. For the second time that morning, the relative tranquillity of Nugent's office was interrupted by the sickening thud of nose-bone and gristle greeting floor.

You can probably guess the sequence from now on. Edward comes round just in time to witness

Nugent hitting the floor. He drags him to a chair, and brings him round just as Nugent's nose also explodes into glorious Technicolor.

Now, blood may be thicker than water, but not by much, and no amount of tightly cupped hands and hastily re-deployed tea towels and ash trays could stop it showing off its liquid qualities to the fullest.

They had started the morning as mere doctor and patient - now suddenly they were elevated to the status of stunt-men in a Quentin Tarantino movie.

Nugent jumps up, screaming. Edward screams back. They grapple to calm each other, but neither had banked on the extra hazard of a blood-soaked linoleum floor, which was now doing a passable impersonation of an ice-rink. Suddenly there's a cartoon-style flurry of Bambi legs and they come crashing to the ground in a tangled heap, savagely banging heads in the process. But this time, with the dubious benefit of consciousness, the impact was felt in full, and they let out a howling unison cry of pain. Both men were seriously considering the option of fainting again, as the only civilized way out of their dilemma, when the two burly security guards burst in.

CHAPTER EIGHT

You couldn't blame the guards. You'd have done much the same in their position. Alerted by the din, they crashed through the office door only to be greeted by the two protagonists yelping in pain, writhing on the floor in a pool of their own blood - in the red corner, the well-respected Doctor Edward Nugent; in the other red corner, the destitute they had spotted earlier drooped suspiciously across his doorway. No competition.

It was the work of seconds to deliver an anaesthetizing blow to the destitute's cranium with a torch, drag him out into the corridor by his feet, and alert the police.

It took over three hours to unravel the facts, bandage the wounded, disinfect the floor and sort out the paperwork. By the time the police had finally, and reluctantly, walked away from the scene empty-handed, it was nearly lunchtime. Not that Edward was feeling hungry. His appetite for life in general had been put on hold ever since Nugent's disturbing voice-mail, and here he was, some seventy-two hours later, still no wiser about his fate.

But that was about to change. As the last of the law enforcement officers finally edged out of Nugent's office with a defiant "I know you two are up to something but I can't prove it" type of backwards glance, the door clicked shut, and the two men were once again alone.

A pale and embarrassed Nugent was the first to speak.

"Edward…erm, first of all…well, sorry about the nose."

"Yours or mine?"

"I meant yours. Why - is mine bad?"

"I've seen better."

"But not on yourself."

"Not right now, no."

"Anyway, I'm sorry. Thing is, I've never been any good at dealing with blood."

"But you're a doctor."

"I'm a hair doctor. Hair doesn't bleed. Just the way I am, I'm afraid. I daren't look, in case I go again. Tell me, has it…stopped?"

"Yes. Just keep your head up."

"You must think I'm a real wimp."

"No, I just think it's weird. I mean, when you were doing my tests, you took, like…"

"Blood tests. That's different. That's needles. I can deal with that. That's under my control. Everything neatly labelled in glass containers. It's the uncontrolled stuff that gets to me. When it starts…squirting out from…"

Nugent started to slump in his chair. Edward rushed over to fan his face with a paper towel.

"All right! All right. Change the subject. Come on. Think about something nice. Think about… erm…baby puppies."

"Baby puppies?"

"Well, I just thought…"

"I don't like dogs. You can't control dogs…"

"All right, let's talk about me instead. Why don't you just…tell me what you've got to tell me. And don't hold back. I know."

Nugent jumped from his seat as if he'd sat on a hot drawing pin. "Know? Know what? What do you know?"

"I know that something is wrong with me. Something very…significant."

There was a moment's eerie silence as Nugent stared out of the window, gathering his thoughts. Edward decided to stay firmly planted in his chair, conscious of the fact that if he stood up he might be asked to sit down, and if were asked to sit down he might panic, and the whole charade would begin again.

Nugent coughed a private, dry cough, and slowly turned to speak. As he did, a strange, unexpected, liberating sense of calm began to flow through Edward's veins. For nearly three days, blind fear had been voraciously consuming vast reserves of his mental energy. Finally, the long wait over, here he was at the emotional point of sale, and he found he simply had nothing left to give. He had total fear fatigue. In short, he was thoroughly prepared for the worst. Nothing could hurt him now, except possibly a sharp prod around the nose area.

His whole body relaxed. He even smiled - perhaps not visibly, but inside he smiled a gentle, knowing smile - and he looked up.

Nugent's lips were parting. Here goes.

Nugent dried. He took a deep breath, and sat down again. And then he stood up again. Sensing Nugent's distress, Edward bravely forced his smile outwards, making sure that Nugent couldn't miss it. He wanted to signal that it was okay for the doctor to deliver his bad news. It was a smile that said he was well-prepared for the worst, and he wouldn't shoot the messenger.

Nugent received the signal loud and clear. The mental rehearsals were over. He knew the time had finally come for him to take centre-stage and deliver his keynote speech.

"Significant. Right. Yes. That's a very apt word, Edward. Significant. Mmm."

Nugent sucked in another hugely exaggerated

deep breath. Any more like that and he would start to affect nearby barometers. "Edward…"

"I'm still here…"

"When I did my tests, I was very thorough - blood samples, DNA, the whole caboodle. I was looking for reasons why your hair had started to grow back. I knew that, if I could understand the process, then maybe I could replicate it, artificially. And if I could do that, well, frankly, the potential is….but you know all this. That's why you came to me."

Edward sensed that Nugent was preparing to deliver the story in weekly instalments, and attempted to move the action along a little.

"So did you find the reason?"

"Yes I did."

"And?"

"And it was not what I was expecting. To be honest, I was expecting that the cause may be linked to blood flow through tiny capillaries in the…."

Torture. Edward, a man already late for an urgent appointment with his fate, had chosen a taxi driver determined to give him a guided tour of all the back streets and blind allies. For the sake of his own sanity, he had to intervene.

"Erm…Ted. Doctor. Mr Nugent. Look…I don't want to appear ungrateful. But please don't tell me what you were expecting. Not yet. Perhaps you can tell me that later. I've been crawling the walls since

Friday night, and right now, with your permission, I'd very much like you to tell me what it is, not what it isn't."

Nugent stopped in his tracks, looking slightly offended, then acknowledged Edward's frustration with a gentle nod.

"The problem is, Edward, I don't think you'd believe me if I told you."

"Try me."

"Very well. But I'm not even sure I believe it myself. Losing hair is a natural part of the ageing process in men, like going grey, or wrinkly. The reason your hair has come back is that…is that…"

"Go on. I can take it."

"Is that in your body, Edward, the ageing process appears to have…stopped."

"Stopped?"

"More than stopped, actually. Gone into reverse."

"I'm not with you."

"There are a thousand and one indicators of ageing, Edward. For example, DNA mutations are more likely the older a cell is, simply because every time a cell divides it is vulnerable to damage, and older cells will have undergone more divisions. Now, most cells are programmed to reproduce a fixed number of times and then die by a sort of cell suicide, a process we call apoptosis. Apoptosis can also be triggered abnormally by certain types of

DNA mutation…"

"Woah! Hold it right there!" Edward intervened with all the vigour of a Hollywood cowboy holding up a stagecoach. "Look - I wasn't with you before, remember? Am I suddenly supposed to be with you if you start spouting on about DNA mutations and cell division and apoplexy and stuff?"

Nugent offered a confused and flustered apology. "Sorry. It's to do with cell damage and…you see we can measure this sort of stuff quite accurately now and, well, the samples you gave me the first week, compared to the samples from the second week… look - here, look at this graph…"

"No!" Edward pleaded for clarity. "Don't give me graphs. Give me facts. Give me a simple sentence."

"Simple's hard!" snapped Nugent, who was now even beginning to frustrate himself. "Look, the science is a little complicated, but the facts are undeniable. In a nutshell, Edward…"

"Yes, that would be nice. Give it me in a nutshell. A nice, tiny, bite-sized nutshell."

Another huge preparatory intake of breath from Nugent. His inhalations were now in danger of affecting the local weather forecast.

"Okay. In a nutshell, then. Here goes. You are, Edward Jones, as far as I can ascertain, doing what no other human being in the history of, well, of human beings, has ever done before. Or animals. Or plants…"

"What sort of nut is this?" screamed Edward. "A coconut? Give me a peanut!"

"All right! In a word, you are, to all intents and purposes..."

"A word! You said in a word!"

"Getting younger!"

Nugent thought it wise to pause for a moment, while the gist of his bombshell in a nutshell sank in. It didn't.

"I'm still not with you."

"No, I'm not really surprised. Edward, how old are you?"

"Forty-five."

"I don't think so."

"What?"

"I don't dispute that you were born forty-five years ago. But when was the last time you looked in a mirror?"

"This weekend."

"And did you see a man of forty-five? Or did you see what I see - a man in his mid-thirties?"

"Well...I..."

"Edward, I have found indisputable scientific evidence that your whole metabolism is operating in reverse. Your hair is growing back because you are getting younger instead of older. It's my guess that this has been happening for at least the past five years. It's not just your hair. It's every cell in your body."

Edward said nothing. He just stared at Nugent - a huge, complex, bewildered stare. Nugent stared back at Edward - a sympathetic, exhausted, I totally understand your need to stare at me in that complex, bewildered way sort of stare. Neither felt it appropriate to say anything else for five whole minutes. Finally, Edward broke the ice with a simple elegance.

"How do I know you're not just talking bollocks?"

"You don't."

"Who else have you told about this?"

"No-one."

"So you could be wrong."

"Possibly. Probably. But I don't see how. I've been over the results a thousand times."

Another long, deep silence. Edward's brow was now furrowed so deep you could have planted potatoes in it. He screwed up his eyes as if he were about to toss them in a wastepaper bin, and aimed them at Nugent.

"So, if I'm getting younger - well, that's good news - isn't it?"

"Erm…up to a point."

"Up to a point? What do you mean? What point?

It's everyone's dream, right? I'm not going to get older, and weaker. I'm getting younger, and stronger."

Nugent slowly turned away to face the window. "Edward, can you remember what you did yesterday?"

"Of course I can, why?"

"And the day before?"

"Yes."

"So your memory's fine?"

"Yes. What's my memory got to do with it?"

"Oh, everything, unfortunately." Nugent wheeled round. "Yes, on the face of it, what you say is true. Getting younger is everyone's dream. How many times have we all wished we were ten years' younger? But you see, even though your body has gone into reverse, your mind hasn't. You remember yesterday, and the day before, which means that your mind - your psychology - is moving forwards, acquiring experience and knowledge in the normal manner, chronologically. Put simply, your body is getting younger, but your mind is still getting older. If this continues - and I'm not saying it will - but if it does, then physically you'll be thirty again, twenty-five again, twenty. But your mind...your personality, will be fifty, fifty-five, sixty. Can't you see?"

Edward, gradually realizing that his imminent death sentence had been lifted, suddenly felt in combative mood. "Yes, I can see. You're saying I get another crack at youth, but with all the benefit of knowledge and experience. That's brilliant."

"Brilliant? Yes, maybe. As I say, up to a point. I suspect there may some good times ahead for you, some amazing times. But think it through, Edward. Think about the psychological impact. You're going to need counselling."

"Counselling? Don't be ridiculous. I'll be on cloud nine."

"But your wife, your friends - they'll all be going the other way. Edward, you'll have no permanent companionship."

"I can live with that. I've always been a bit of a loner."

"You'll need to be. Because one day, you're going to find yourself to be an old-age pensioner in a teenager's body."

"Great. I'll be the ultimate dirty old man."

"Do you really want to go back to school when you're sixty-five?"

"I won't need school. I'll be educated."

"And what happens when you're a toddler?"

"I'll just stay at home and play with my toys. The perfect retirement."

"And who'll be your mom when you're three?"

"Who cares, I…"

"And what happens three years later?"

Now it was Edward's turn to be stopped in his tracks. Nugent had presented him with an extraordinary series of rapid-fire thoughts and images, all of which had left Edward dazed but excited. But this last one had hit him right between the eyes. It's one thing to tackle your birthdays in descending order, but quite another to consciously face the mother of all birthdays - the actual day of your birth - from the wrong end of the womb. How does that work? It's not like he has anywhere to go. He'd be an old man, trapped in the body of a baby, waiting for what? Death? What sort of death? Would he celebrate his eightieth year, his final birthday party, in an incubator, shrinking, waiting for a nine-month reduction back into a sperm? And beyond the sperm, where to next?

Edward's jaw had dropped so far that Nugent could have reached in and grabbed his tonsils. But he saw no mileage in this. Instead, he opted to pat Edward gently on the shoulder, and pulled up a chair beside him. Once again, the two men sat in total silence for what seemed like an eternity.

Finally, Edward's desperately tired eyes lifted their intense gaze from the floor and began deeply scanning Nugent's face for signs of comfort. Nugent put his arm around him, and offered a faint smile.

It would have been a deeply touching and serious moment, had Edward not been distracted by the activities of Nugent's enflamed nose. He suddenly noticed that it had a pulse. He could actually see it throbbing. And Nugent, almost telepathically, had simultaneously homed in on Edward's equally gigantic and equally pulsating conk. They looked like two disappointed runners-up in a Jimmy Durante look-alike boxing competition.

One smile became two, two smiles exploded into broad grins, and there was a brief moment of comic relief, red noses and all.

Nugent took his cue from the break in tension.

"Look, Edward...let me just say, I am sure about my findings. But what I'm not sure about - in fact what I have no idea about whatsoever - is why this happened, or whether it will last, or if it can be reversed. I was hoping to brief you on this in a more controlled fashion, but..."

"The lightning."

"What?"

"I was struck by lightning. Five years ago. My fortieth birthday. Everybody said I was lucky to survive. That's when it all started. I'm sure it is."

"Lightning?"

"A bolt from the blue."

As Nugent's face absorbed this precious new data, he went so deep into thought that he slipped into an altered state of consciousness. Edward, noticing that his companion was no longer willing to take part in any meaningful dialogue, waved a hand in front of his face and asked him if he was all right, but it was no use. Nugent had clearly locked himself away and slipped a huge 'Do Not Disturb' sign over his eyes. Edward sensed that something quite vital was happening, and decided to respect his privacy.

It was two whole minutes before Nugent re-appeared.

"Edward," he said, still staring three thousand miles through and beyond the floorboards, "I'm about to ask you the most difficult question imaginable, and I need an answer."

"If it's algebra, forget it," quipped Edward, and then immediately wished he hadn't. Nugent's only reaction to this half-baked attempt to lighten the mood was to fix his patient with the sort of withering stare you'd reserve for an irksome dung beetle. Edward got the message, and lowered his eyes in shame. "Go on," he mumbled.

"If I could find a way, do you want me to reverse this?"

"Can it be done?"

"Possibly. But you're going to need to be incredibly brave."

Nugent's words pierced Edward's body like a thousand red-hot needles. This was supposed to be the end of his emotional rollercoaster ride. Now, all he could hear was the ominous metallic clatter of the chain, as he was slowly winched up to the highest point of the track, ready to face its devastating climax.

Edward swallowed hard and turned away. Suddenly, uncontrollably, horribly, his body gave way to every clichéd symptom of fear at once.

Cold sweat was breaking out on his brow, using moisture which was presumably being siphoned directly from his mouth. He felt his heart thumping on his chest wall like an angry neighbour wanting the music turned down. His knees, once standard-issue bone and gristle, were rapidly turning into a pair of knee-shaped jellies. His stomach was a lepidopterist's dream. And his bowels - well, you don't want to know about his bowels.

The reason for this sudden and desperate descent into blind panic was clear. For the last forty-eight hours, Edward Jones had already been the bravest man he thought himself capable of being. And now, it seemed, he was being told that his trials were only just beginning.

Quite how he managed to turn and deliver his next line he didn't know.

"What do I have to do?" he croaked.

"Come with me," said Nugent. "I have a theory."

CHAPTER NINE

Sarah Appleby was out walking her dog when her house exploded.

It was a lucky escape - five minutes earlier she was in the kitchen, attempting to attach the lead to the dog collar. If her spaniel had been its normal unruly self, both master and canine companion would have ended up scattered across the nearby fields in kit form.

Fortunately, Sarah lived in a detached residence in an extremely secluded spot, or the carnage would have been sickening. Even from just over a mile away, a fragment of one of Sarah's bathroom tiles managed to land on her head, and the bang was heard in the neighbouring village by a man who, until that point, was convinced that he was deaf.

In short, it was a big explosion.

Nothing remained of the house except a black, smoking dent in the ground. The television aerial, which had always leaned a few degrees from the vertical, was instantly launched like a sky rocket and claimed the only casualty, a passing crow, harpooning it to an oak tree.

For those that knew Sarah, none of this was a surprise. They were only shocked she'd gone this long without some sort of major catastrophe, and it was no coincidence that she lived so remotely.

Sarah, you see, liked to experiment.

Ever since she was a toddler, she'd been strangely intrigued by all things scientific. While other little girls were out playing hopscotch, Sarah would be in her bedroom, randomly mixing together the sort of chemicals that came out of padlocked lead containers marked with a skull and crossbones, just to see what would happen. And if nothing particularly exciting resulted, she would try applying a naked flame, or an electrical current, just to spice up the evening.

Sarah's activities first achieved notoriety many years ago, when her grandmother, halfway through wishing her old friend Mrs Rickets a very merry Christmas, spontaneously combusted in the supermarket. It made all the local papers. She only avoided serious injury thanks to the quick-thinking actions of a young boy who was about to put a soda siphon in his mother's trolley. The incident baffled police and scientists alike, until it was eventually discovered that old ma Appleby had accidentally sipped one of Sarah's potions instead of her Yuletide sherry at the family party, and this had caused her to become unstable.

Young Sarah was given a stern warning by the local bobby that she must never again do whatever it was she'd done. Meanwhile, her flammably-challenged grandmother, who had escaped with little more than dampened pride and a soggy perm, went stoically marching on to the ripe old age of a hundred and seven. But the mould was set. (Incidentally, talking of moulds, the young boy with the soda siphon, clearly inspired by his success, went on to join the fire brigade. Give me a child until he is seven, and I'll show you the man.)

To the locals, Sarah was nothing more or less than a witch, and not even a white one at that. But this was a slightly simplistic view of her career. She did these days, after all, apparently hold some sort of official Government licence to legally pursue her mysterious activities - even, it was rumoured by the conspiracy theorists in the village, getting secret funding from MI5. But if there was any form of legitimate endgame to her clandestine experiments, it had surely now suffered a major setback.

As soon as Sarah saw the blinding flash of light, followed a second later by the ear-splitting shriek of a thousand harpies - as soon as the tidal wave of foul-smelling air thumped into her chest, sending her sprawling backwards over her whimpering dog - she knew she had a problem. The fragment of tile which beaned her twenty seconds later was merely confirmation of the obvious. The experiment had gone slightly wrong.

Little point going home, she reasoned, as home

was now clearly visible against the evening sky, in the form of a fabulous meteor shower, so she set off in the direction of her nearest neighbour, some two miles East across the common, in order to make a telephone call.

As she trudged despondently through the mud, Sarah reflected on what might have been. She felt sure that this time she'd cracked it. Her early experiments on fruit flies had been so promising - she'd managed to extend their life three-fold by making them pass through a fluctuating magnetic field in order to reach their food, which consisted of a secret blend of seven herbs and spices, some genetically modified vitamins, and a special extract from over-ripe bananas.

In fact, the head fruit fly, affectionately known as Ronald, seemed to be thriving on the experiment, and was approaching the human equivalent of five hundred years old when he suddenly and without warning swelled up to the size of a tennis ball and exploded into a mist of yellow sticky vapour.

Sarah had played back the CCTV footage in slow motion hundreds of times and was still no closer to a satisfactory explanation. A post-mortem was not really practical, as all the evidence now resided on a kitchen towel. Rather like Sarah's dear departed grandmother, something had made the fruit fly temporarily unstable - either the increased banana dosage, or the latest tweak in the computer's magnetic fluctuation pattern - possibly a complex combination of both.

Ronald's unfortunate demise had put the human trials back another month or two, but nevertheless Sarah's work still attracted huge interest from the pharmaceutical companies, who for some reason saw the development of a magic elixir offering eternal youth as a potential money-spinner.

The problem for Sarah, however, had always been scaling her experiments up to more advanced species. There was no real way of testing if you'd dramatically increased the lifespan of, say, a dog, without hanging around for thirty or forty years. And should it ultimately prove a failure, no self-respecting dog fed day and night on banana extract was likely to thank you for improving the overall quality of its existence.

Fruit flies, on the other hand, seemed to have no real problems with the banana diet (apart from the occasional swelling up and exploding incident) and their normal life span of little more than three score hours and ten meant there was plenty of scope to mess around with the ingredients to see what yielded the best results. Trouble is, the market for fruit fly life enhancement is, at best, niche. Let's face it, none of the pharmaceutical giants were ultimately battling it out to get a bigger share of the fruit fly wallet. In pragmatic terms, the gratitude of an old fruit fly, no matter how touching, was no match for the human dollar.

And there were other frustrations. Ridiculously bureaucratic regulations governing new medicines meant that Sarah was unlikely to get approval to introduce a procedure which might possibly lead to the occasional human exploding into a yellow mist. Idiots. Can't they see?

In short then, until Sarah could make the scientific leap from achieving encouraging but unpredictable results with drosophila melanogaster (fruit flies), to proven and consistent success with homo sapiens (blokes), she would only ever find herself on a modest retainer. Small comfort to a woman with no house. The main prize, therefore, still eluded her.

At last. A cottage, and signs of life. A neatly trimmed pair of topiary peacocks greeted Sarah and her dog as they walked up the gravel driveway of the elegant country retreat. Neat, that is, except for the fact that one of the peacocks was missing its head.

Sarah leant down to comfort her dog as she tied his lead to a conveniently situated drainpipe.

"Sorry, Jack - I'll have to leave you here. They wouldn't understand."

Now, I know what you're thinking. 'What wouldn't they understand about a dog?' Well, at this point I need to hold up my hands. If you believe that the writer's prime duty is to paint a mental picture for the reader, I think I might just have blown it.

I failed to mention that Sarah's dog was invisible.

I know, I know, serious omission and all that, and I really am sorry - particularly if you're the sort of conscientious reader that likes to visualize the action frame by frame, and now feels obliged to go back to five pages and start all over again. But you can see my dilemma, even if you can no longer see the dog. This isn't the sort of information you can just toss out at will. It takes time to sink in. And it begs all sorts of questions, such as 'Why is Sarah's dog invisible?' and the equally vexing 'How is Sarah's dog invisible?'

All I can do is ask for your patience. Everything will, in time, make a sort of sense.

Sarah gave a respectful rat-tat-tat on the front door. Almost immediately the lounge curtains flicked open, and an elderly man with extraordinary eyebrows peered out into the night. He squinted into the dimly-lit porch, trying to assess whether his visitor was friend or foe, and then disappeared back behind the drapes. A few moments later, on came the hall light, and the silhouette of a gigantic stick insect with furry head wings approached the glass-panelled door. It could have been Hermes. It wasn't, though, it was Mr Rogers.

"Who's there?"

"Erm…it's Sarah Appleby, from across the common. I was wondering if I could use your phone, only…mine's not working."

The door creaked open tentatively, and one of Rogers' eyebrows slowly emerged into the night, closely followed by its owner. He gave his visitor a cautious once-over.

"Sarah Appleby – from Grange Lane?"

"That's me."

Rogers' eyebrows twitched, and his face relaxed into a broad, welcoming grin. "I've heard a good deal about you."

"Yes, I bet you have."

"Oh, don't you worry, my dear. I don't believe in such superstitious nonsense. Well, come in, do."

"Thank you."

Rogers darted a glance around Sarah's feet as she entered. "Erm...on your own?"

"Yes, why?"

"Oh. So that wasn't your dog I heard barking just now?"

Sarah smiled sweetly. "No, witches only have black cats."

Rogers enjoyed the quip. "Yes. Yes, so you do."

As the front door closed, an invisible spaniel chose the perfect moment to call after its master.

"I think your cat just barked again."

Sarah reprised her sweet smile, this time a little more nervously, and without the back-up of a decent one-liner. Luckily, Rogers didn't pursue the point.

"Trouble with your phone, you say?"

"Yes, it's erm...well, it stopped working when my house exploded."

"Exploded? Good Lord. That wasn't your bang I heard a few minutes ago, was it?"

"Fraid so. One of my experiments appears to have, well, back-fired."

"Is the house badly hurt?"

"Oh, I don't think it felt a thing. Completely evaporated."

"Goodness me. My dear girl, by all means. Whom did you want to phone?"

"Well, just a local hotel for now. I'll, erm, start picking up the pieces tomorrow, when it's light."

"How dreadful for you. But look, I've got a spare room here - least I can do is give you shelter for the night."

"Well, I don't want to be any trouble…"

"No trouble at all."

"Well, that's…fantastic - thank you."

"Not at all. Darling?"

Rogers suddenly bellowed to another invisible companion - his wife Muriel.

"Darling! We have a visitor. She's staying the night. Miss…Appletree did you say?"

"Sarah."

"Miss Sarah. Her house has exploded and she needs shelter."

Sarah thought she heard some sort of muffled

reply from upstairs, but she couldn't be sure. For all she knew, Mrs Rogers was gagged and tied to the bed, and Mr Rogers was a lunatic. She'd seen films like that.

"This is very kind of you."

"Not at all, not at all. Come in, take a seat. My wife will be down presently, I'm sure. She has trouble with her feet these days. Now then, whisky, port, sherry - or would you prefer tea?"

"Oh, well. Erm…whisky's fine."

"Excellent. There we are, then. Well, Miss Appletree - or may I call you Suzie?"

"Erm…yes, Suzie's fine."

"Well, Suzie - call me a nosy old parker if you like, but I take quite a bit of interest in science myself, and if you've got the time and the energy, I'd love to hear all about your experiments."

CHAPTER TEN

Nugent was a good man. One of the best. But even he occasionally let standards slip when it came to the basic business of sooth-saying. In short, he'd told a fib. He had, after all, clearly indicated to Edward that he'd told no-one about his dramatic findings.

Let's review the evidence:

Edward: "How do I know you're not just talking bollocks?"

Nugent: "You don't."

Edward: "Who else have you told about this?"

Nugent: "No-one."

No escaping the facts, then. Those are the words, verbatim, straight from the court stenographer. At the time, it felt like the right thing to say. Trouble is, everyone knows at least one person they can trust with a secret ("Don't breathe a word of this to a soul, but…") and consequently the troubled Nugent had confided in his wife, Agnes.

Agnes, of course, wouldn't dream of telling a

soul, so she was careful to warn her friend Brenda that she mustn't tell a soul. Not that Brenda would dream of breathing a word of it to anyone except her best friend, Clara. Clara, sworn to secrecy, made sure that she only told people she could trust to keep a secret. And those she told only passed it on to those whom they trusted not to pass it on to anyone who would pass it on to anyone who would pass it on.

Thus it was that, eight days later, the greatest secret of the modern world hit the front pages of the tabloids.

It was Friday, 7am. Edward was in the shower when the doorbell rang. Mary answered the door to a steaming, throbbing confusion of reporters, all thrusting microphones and cameras into her face, all talking at once. She was more than a tad bewildered, as she never read newspapers.

To add to the cacophony and chaos, the phone was also ringing in a way which, though it defied logic, definitely sounded far more urgent than a normal phone ring. Mary, wide-eyed and clueless, slammed the door on the jabbering mass and answered it. It was Martin, her son, who'd just picked up the first edition of the Daily Star, closely followed by his jaw.

"Mom! What the hell's going on?"

"Oh, Martin! I don't know. There are millions of reporters outside."

"I'm not surprised. Have you read the papers?"

"No. What about?"

"About dad!"

"Oh my God! What's he done? Don't tell me he's had an affair."

There was a small pause while Martin practised looking nonplussed. "Mom, with all due respect, dad's sexual adventures are hardly likely to excite the interests of the paparazzi."

"What then?"

"So you don't know?"

"Know what?"

"Stay put. Don't talk to anyone. Keep the door locked. I'm on my way."

And he was gone.

This left Mary feeling perplexed, with a capital F. Outside, three hundred reporters, doing a passable impersonation of three thousand reporters, beating down her door. Upstairs, whistling obliviously in the shower, her husband of twenty-four years, who'd done something. She knew not what. Just something…well, big. In fact, something huge. In fact, something… (a quick flick of the curtains just to check she wasn't day-dreaming…no, she wasn't, they're now trampling on the lawn and banging their microphones and cameras on the lounge window)…something positively humungous. And, if she knew newspapers, which she didn't (except what they said about newspapers on the television) he'd more than likely done something really bad.

Robbed a bank. Mugged an old lady. Offended the Queen. Not paid his taxes since he was six. Or worse, not paid them since he was five.

Whatever it was, she didn't know about it, and the heaving swarm outside did. Do swarms heave? Who cares? The fact is, hell hath no fury like a woman whose husband is upstairs whistling in a shower while hundreds of nosy reporters who know what he's done are gathered outside her front door.

The phone rings again. This time it's an even tetchier ring, like a phone with PMT that doesn't want to be disturbed. Mary grabs the lifeline, thinking it must be Martin again. It isn't. The voice on the other end sounds even more agitated than she does.

"Edward?"

"Do I sound like Edward?" snapped Mary.

"Sorry - I can't hear very well - too much noise."

"That's because all your lot are banging down my door!"

"My lot?"

"Reporters. Don't tell me you're not one of them!"

"I'm not one of them."

"Hah!"

"Mrs Jones…is that Mrs Jones?"

"It might be. Who are you?"

"Mrs Jones, I'm not a reporter. They're here as well - at my house. I'm Nugent."

"What?"

"Nugent!"

"A newsagent?"

"I'm a doctor, Mrs Jones. Doctor Nugent. The man that's been helping your husband."

"Helping him what?"

"Hasn't he told you?"

"No."

"Oh. Haven't you read the papers?"

"No."

"Oh. Is your husband there, please?"

"He's in the shower."

"It's very urgent."

"He's still in the shower."

"Bring him to the phone - please - it's vital I talk to him."

No need. As Mary looks up, a soggy Edward, draped in nothing but a towel and a look of total astonishment, is standing at the bottom of the stairs.

"What the bloody hell's going on, Mary?"

"I thought you might tell me. Here!" she snapped, thrusting him the phone. "Talk to your friend. I'm going to make the ham sandwiches."

Even in a crisis, Mary was a creature of strict habit. Edward tentatively placed the receiver to his dripping ear.

"Hello?"

"Edward. It's Ted. Don't ask me how, but the cat's out of the bag. Your story's all over the front pages."

"What?"

"Listen to these headlines: The Sun: **Medical Freak Defies Ageing Process**. The Mirror leads with **The Incredible Shrinking Man**. The Guardian: **Real-Life Dorian Gray Shocks the World**."

"But who told them?"

"Not me. But this is big, Edward. Out of control. My office has been broken into. All my notes have been stolen. We have to meet."

"Where?"

"The park opposite the hospital. Can you slip out without being followed?"

Edward took a sneaky look outside through a slit in the curtains. Something instinctively told him that strolling out through the front door whistling was unlikely to meet the brief. His eyes narrowed. "I'll find a way," he said.

Edward Jones. Boring Edward Jones. Edward, wouldn't say 'boo' to a goose, holiday in a caravan, never go out on a Saturday night, Jones. Here he was, disguised as his wife, climbing out of an upstairs back bedroom window to escape the world's press, hot-wiring his neighbour's car and rushing off to a clandestine meeting with a doctor who had recently told him he was five years' younger than he was five years ago. Not so boring now, eh? How many others could say that's how they started their Friday mornings?

Friday? Oh, bugger. In his haste to slip down the drainpipe he'd forgotten his ham sandwiches. He hated forgetting his sandwiches. They were already made, too, neatly cling-wrapped and waiting by the kitchen door. What a waste.

Mary, meanwhile, still besieged by the mob, was searching the house for Edward, determined to get to the bottom of all this before he left for work. What she eventually found was not Edward, but an opened bedroom window, and a hastily ransacked wardrobe. Her wardrobe.

Yes, they were her clothes that Edward had left strewn all over the bed. But not all of them. The red trouser suit was missing.

The awful truth suddenly hit her. She lay down on the bed and cried herself to sleep.

*　　*　　*

She woke with a start. A hand was touching her.

"Mom. It's only me."

"Martin!"

"It's all right. I've told them all to bugger off. I've told them no-one's talking, and that dad's not here."

"He's not. He escaped."

She pointed woefully towards the open window. Martin closed it and sat beside her.

"Have you seen the papers yet?" he asked.

"No," Mary replied tearfully. "But I know."

"It's unbelievable, isn't it."

"Over twenty years together, Martin. And never once did I get a hint of it."

"Yeah, well, it only started a few years ago, apparently."

"But why?"

"Nobody seems to know. One paper said it was something to do with him being hit by lightning."

"That's ridiculous."

"Jolted his metabolism or something."

Mary's trembling bottom lip finally gave way to a flood of tears. Martin, never quite comfortable in the comforting department, gently patted her head.

"Come on, mom…"

"It's me, isn't it? I've caused all this."

"Don't be daft, mom. How could you have caused it?"

"I'm not stupid, Martin…" (Martin didn't have time to intervene) "…A man doesn't suddenly start dressing up in women's clothes unless there's something missing at home."

Martin's hand patted its last pat. There was a moment's silence while he rewound his internal tape just to check the last few moments of dialogue. Yes, she'd said it all right. Better play safe and get proper clarification.

"Er…what do you mean, mom?"

"Well, there are plenty of transvestites out there, Martin. You can't tell me they've all been struck by lightning."

Okay. It was now clear that Martin and his mom were operating in parallel universes. If there was to be any genuine communication from now on, one of them had to make the inter-galactic journey into the other's mind. Martin decided it had better be him, as he was the youngest and fittest.

"What the bloody hell are you going on about, mom?"

Mary tearfully re-traced her steps, explaining how she'd made Edward's ham sandwiches, placed them by the kitchen door, searched the house for him, and finally discovered the missing outfit and the open window. She'd put two and two together and managed to make four to the power of ten.

Martin didn't quite know where to start. He was, however, instinctively confident that his dad hadn't suddenly turned to cross-dressing. It didn't need

Sherlock Holmes to deduce that he'd probably just ad-libbed with his mother's wardrobe in order to avoid the urgent attentions of the press.

Mary had always been on the frail side, emotionally. And she'd already condensed her entire decade's quota of shocks into the last few hours, so Martin had to tread carefully if he wasn't going to send her off into one of her hysterical spasms. He'd witnessed a number of such spasms in the Jones' household over the years, and they didn't make a pleasant spectator sport. Apart from being grotesquely shrill, to the point where they could upturn dogs and bring down passing bats, they also seemed to be entirely unpredictable - he remembered one in particular which appeared to have no other catalyst than a burnt fish finger - but what he did know was that, once they were triggered, nothing short of a bucket of iced water over the head followed by a hearty slapping would do the trick.

He began with the good news. He was reasonably sure that his dad - her husband of twenty-odd years - wasn't a transvestite. Even if he were, it would hardly be enough to excite the local corner shop gossips, let alone the world's press. The red trouser suit was a red herring - a disguise - to throw the reporters off the scent. Of this he was certain. Well, certain-ish.

Okay - so far, so good. Though she was still blubbing, Mary seemed comparatively heartened by Martin's confidence, and she was definitely beginning to show signs of buying the disguise explanation. Now came the tricky bit. If it wasn't his cross-dressing habits that the reporters were interested in, what was it? Martin tried jump-starting his spluttering explanation with a "You see, mom…" followed by a "To cut a long story short, mom…" and he even tossed in a quick "Well, basically, mom…" but nothing quite seemed to hit the spot.

In the end, he simply plucked a creased-up copy of the Daily Star from his pocket and handed it to her.

"Here," he said. "Read it for yourself."

CHAPTER ELEVEN

Ted Nugent was pacing up and down by the park railings like a neurotic caged tiger.

Six paces, turn, six paces, turn. After just a few minutes he'd already worn a noticeable groove in the soft ground. Had Edward shown up a few hours later than he did, he would have found Nugent peeping out from a trench.

In an impromptu tribute to his childhood heroes Starsky & Hutch, Edward bounced up the kerb by the park gates and screeched his neighbour's borrowed vehicle to a dramatic halt. He recognized Nugent at once, even though the eminent doctor was wearing a frock and furry hat.

"Edward! Thank goodness you had the sense to come in disguise," Nugent squeaked hoarsely. "These people are everywhere. We can't talk here. Come on."

Nugent marched Edward to a remote bench in the centre of the park, scanned the horizon anxiously, and then proceeded to communicate in an urgent stage whisper.

"We mustn't draw attention to ourselves."

"Oh, that's all right then," Edward snorted. "Two transvestite six-footers dressed for a wedding shouldn't draw much of a crowd."

"Here." Nugent delved into his handbag and slipped Edward a round of stale bread. Edward pounced, stuffing it into his mouth like a ravenous escaped convict.

"Thanks. I'm bloody starving."

"It's not for you!" barked Nugent. "Feed the ducks."

Edward sulkily ripped the excess bread strips from around his mouth and began flicking them grudgingly at the waiting wildlife. Nugent resumed his over-dramatic squeaky whisper, sounding more and more like a pubescent choir boy. "Do you think you were followed?"

"I'm not sure. One car did look a bit suspicious, but…."

"But what?"

"Well, he was in front of me."

Nugent grunted his general dissatisfaction, and then continued to work on his impersonation of an expectant caged tiger. "This is crazy, Edward. I don't know how it could have leaked out."

"Well don't look at me," Edward retorted indignantly. "I didn't even tell my wife."

"Well neither did…" Nugent stopped pacing. His

eyes widened. "All right, what's done's done. We need to find a way out of this mess. Nice trouser suit, by the way."

"Thank you."

"Red suits you."

The last thing either man wanted at that moment was to be approached by the park drunk offering them money for sex. But what we want and what we get are often opposite poles.

"Hiya, girlsh!" The foul-smelling and slurred words had to find their way through a gap in the tramp's black front teeth, which added a curious whistling sound to virtually every syllable. "Fanshy a goodsh time, ladiesh? Eh? Cosh I've'sh got shum moneysh, look!" He ferreted in his pocket and produced a bent French franc.

Strangely enough, neither man was in the mood to take their suitor up on his generous offer. But the drunk simply wouldn't take "No" - or for that matter "Bugger off" - for an answer. He didn't appear to be too fussy about his quarry, either, though he seemed just on balance to favour the younger-looking Edward, and eventually tried placing a groping hand on his knee. Edward's response, no doubt fuelled by acute stress and a massive adrenalin rush, was a swift and decisive chinning, which sent the drunk skidding headlong down the grassy bank until he eventually came to rest in the water feature.

"Great!" exploded Nugent. "We're supposed to be

trying not to draw attention to ourselves here!"

Edward was unrepentant. "I've been through a lot in the last few weeks, Ted. I'm not having sex with a man just to keep him quiet. Especially one that's been drinking."

"He could have been undercover."

"Well, now he's underwater. Either way, he's out of commission. Come on, let's get out of here."

Nugent edged cautiously towards the pond.

"What the hell are you doing?" screamed Edward, desperate to do a runner.

"I need to check him out," bellowed Nugent.

"Why?"

"I'm a doctor. You might have killed him."

Edward's eyes turned into a pair of saucers. In fact, the only reason they weren't dinner plates is that Edward had recently learnt to handle surprising news.

"Shit! Really?"

"Just make sure nobody's coming."

Edward rushed to the top of the bank and anxiously scanned the horizon while Nugent lifted the drunk's head above the waterline and checked for signs of a pulse. Edward was totally panic-stricken. He'd never thought of himself as a potential killer before, and the longer the drunk lay motionless, the more freaked out he became. In the end, the pressure became unbearable. He deserted his look-out post, rushed to Nugent's side and demanded to know his fate.

"Well?"

"Well, you've doubled the gap in his teeth, and there's a tadpole in his mouth, but other than that no real damage done."

"Thank God for that. I didn't mean to hurt him. Honestly. I only wanted to hit him."

"He'll probably have a bit of a headache in the morning, but I suspect he would have had that anyway. Come on. We need to get out of here before he wakes up."

"Where are we going?"

"I've got an idea. We'll need your car."

"It's not my car," protested Edward.

"Even better."

Nugent's idea was to hide out somewhere remote. A friend's house. A friend Nugent could trust.

Edward flung his neighbour's car dramatically around the country lanes like a man desperately trying to defend a two-second lead in the RAC rally. Nugent, his cross-dressing co-driver, was frantically barking instructions:

"Next left…two hundred yards, fourth gear… sharp right… blind hill, into third, fifty yards…into second, hard left…watch out for that…"

There was a sickening thud. The bonnet of the car sprang up. The engine hissed steam.

"….tree."

"Bollocks!" screamed Edward. "Jim's going to kill me."

"Leave it!" ordered Nugent. "Get the hell out of here before somebody sees us. We can walk the rest."

As they rounded the corner, Edward suddenly recognized the territory. He knew that house. He recognized the gravel drive, those topiary peacocks, that missing head.

"This is Doctor Rogers' house!"

"Yes. We can trust him."

Nugent rapped urgently on the door.

"Strange," he said. "I didn't know he had a dog."

*　　*　　*

Sarah Appleby was in the process of feeding her spaniel in the kitchen. Rogers was upstairs tending to his mysterious wife's feet and, rather than risk letting the barking disturb them, Sarah opened the door.

She didn't expect to see two men dressed in women's clothing. They didn't expect to see someone who wasn't Rogers. There followed a

Mexican stand-off of puzzled expressions.

"Who are you?"

"Who are you?"

(It doesn't really matter who said which bit - the net result's the same.)

"Where's Mr Rogers?" (That was Nugent.)

"He's upstairs. Who shall I say is calling?" (That was Sarah.)

"A friend." (Nugent)

"Two friends." (Edward)

"And hurry up - it's urgent." (Nugent)

"Very well. I will alert Mr Rogers to your presence." (Sarah again, who for reasons best known to herself, had suddenly felt compelled to adopt the vernacular of Jeeves.)

Sarah did not wish to look alarmed, but alarmed is what she felt inside. Why? Well, only a matter of hours ago, she had confided some of her greatest scientific secrets to the genial Mr Rogers. Never before had she talked openly about her work, but something about his host's generosity of spirit, not to mention his generosity with spirits, had loosened Sarah's tongue. In fact, not just loosened it, but practically taken it off its hinges. And, once loosened, it had rattled. Oh, how it had rattled. Like an excited rattlesnake's bottom. Like a hillbilly's unfastened window shutter in a hurricane. Like a really rattly thing that was determined to show off just how rattly it could be in a rattling competition.

The secrets poured out as fast as the whisky. And it had felt good. Liberating. Sarah, who had always ploughed a lonely furrow, had finally found a kindred soul. A man who understood. A man of wisdom. A man who oozed integrity. A man who now had two transvestites calling on him by name.

There's an old adage about not judging a book by its cover. But it doesn't seem to make adequate provision for situations concerning doctors with cross-dressing friends and, as Sarah reached the top of the stairs, she was already working on a last-ditch panic strategy of protecting her trade secrets by blackmailing the respectable Mr Rogers.

Her tactic was simple. "Keep quiet about my fruit flies, and I'll keep quiet about your fruit friends." Yes. It seemed workable enough, until she was given pause by the fact she'd seen more than one film where blackmail had led to murder, and murder had led to death. In this case, hers.

Sarah tapped on the bedroom door. An eyebrow emerged.

"Sorry to interrupt. There are two…gentlemen to see you - downstairs."

"Well, I'm rather tied up at the moment," said the eyebrow.

"They said it was urgent. They said they were friends of yours."

"Oh, right, thank you. Erm…would you mind just

finishing this off for me?"

Rogers handed her the two unresolved ends of an enormous bandage, and disappeared downstairs. Sarah stood perplexed, wondering exactly what "finishing this off" involved. She cautiously traced the origin of the bandages around the door and into the bedroom. They led to an elderly pair of lady's feet, which in turn led to an elderly lady, who was lying flat on her back on the floor, but with her knees propped up high on cushions, like a geriatric astronaut preparing for take off.

Sarah presumed this to be Mrs Rogers, and her bad feet. They were certainly somebody's bad feet, and Mrs R would appear to be in pole position to claim them.

Sarah had obviously heard Rogers mention his wife several times, but somehow, despite having squatted in the same house as her for nearly twenty-four hours, their paths had never actually crossed. In fact, it was a bit of a relief to finally prove her existence, as Sarah was beginning to wonder if Mr Rogers had made her up to keep him company, or perhaps, even more worryingly, had continued talking to his wife and doing her feet long after she'd died. She'd seen films like that as well. Sarah decided to do what the old lady obviously couldn't - put her best foot forward.

"Mrs Rogers, I presume."

"Muriel. And you must be Sarah," replied the outrageously posh old lady. She was definitely one of the old school - the sort that still wore huge pink hats on Sunday. She had an upper lip as stiff as a concrete lintel, and possessed the sort of glorious accent that sounded like she was auditioning for a lead role in a David Lean film.

"Do forgive my prostrate position - my feet aren't as good as they were, you know."

This was a classic British understatement.

Peeping through the unfinished bandaging was the foot equivalent of the Elephant Man. She had a…well, whatever the collective term for giant bunions is - a gaggle, or herd, or something - which had sent her toes spiralling off at all sorts of outrageous angles. Her big toe pointed towards her heel, while the other four each favoured a different point of the compass. And that was not to mention the corns, blisters and the thousand other natural shocks that feet are heir to. In fact, getting any form of footwear to fit her without hand stitching a custom solution for every digit would have been impossible - even a foot spa would rub her. But the poor woman bore her disfiguring disability with fortitude and dignity.

"My husband appears to have dashed orff without finishing the job. Would you mind?"

"Erm…I'm not sure what…"

"Just strap 'em up, good and tight. It'll straighten 'em up eventually. Bit like putting a brace on teeth, you see?"

Sarah didn't see. In fact, she was distinctly

sceptical. The only thing that would straighten those feet was an aggressive session with an electric hedge trimmer. Nor did she relish the task ahead of her. She wasn't a great fan of feet at the best of times - especially other people's - but even the most obsessive foot fetishist would get a tad squeamish faced with the weird mutants now confronting her.

Close up, they looked like something you might have seen in a very early episode of Dr Who, except they were in colour, which made them all the more scary. All in all, it was a grim duty she was being asked to perform. But this was, after all, the lady of the house that had given her such needy shelter, and Sarah thought it might be considered rude if she were to suddenly faint, or vomit, or scream and jump out of the window, and so she sucked in her breath, gritted her teeth and stoically got to work.

Now, the key to dealing with major unpleasantries is to block them from your mind. Fortunately, Sarah didn't find this too difficult. The fact is, even though her hands were upstairs, dealing with feet, her mind was downstairs, wondering what was transpiring between Rogers and his strange music-hall chums. Consequently, even though the up-turned Mrs Rogers was talking virtually non-stop throughout the bandaging session, Sarah heard not a single word. Perhaps the old lady was talking about the weather, or the state of the nation. Perhaps she was giving the foot novice some much-needed advice on the best way to tackle her duties -

Sarah wouldn't know - she'd long since glazed over.

In the absence of any specific directives from her brain, Sarah's arms and hands went in auto-pilot. That's fine when you're on familiar territory, less so when you're doing something for the first time. Whereas a typical foot-bandaging virgin might concentrate and take things slowly, by way of compensating for a general lack of experience, Sarah was flying along like a seasoned professional who was late for another appointment. But, of course, it was all bluff.

As Sarah strutted purposefully out of the bedroom, she was focused on just one thing - eavesdropping on the conversation below. What she'd left behind, stranded on the carpet, may have looked like a giant mummified caterpillar, but it was actually a bewildered old lady whose two legs had been strapped together to form one. Her posh protestations fell on deaf ears.

Meanwhile, downstairs, things were really hotting up.

CHAPTER TWELVE

When Sarah disappeared upstairs to fetch Rogers, Nugent and Edward had decided not to wait for a formal invitation to step over the threshold. Fearful of the press picking up the scent and spotting them lurking on the doorstep, they'd closed and bolted the front door behind them, scuttled into the nearest room, drawn the curtains and taken the phone off the hook.

At first, Rogers assumed that his mystery visitors had simply changed their mind and gone away. But, just as he was about to ascend the stairs and return to his formal duties as Head Footman, he heard urgent mutterings coming from the vicinity of his lounge. He grabbed an umbrella and decided to investigate.

"Peter - thank God you're in. We need help."

It was hard to disagree. There, large as life, sweating and dishevelled on his hearthrug, was one of Rogers' oldest friends, a burly Yorkshireman to boot, dressed rather unconvincingly as Miss Marple. Next to him, another familiar face - he couldn't quite place it - but his many years of medical experience quickly helped Rogers to the conclusion that it too wasn't female. Now, finding one transvestite in your lounge is perhaps a tad unfortunate. Finding two definitely smacks of carelessness. Something wasn't right. In fact, several things weren't right. Rogers decided to hang on to the umbrella for insurance.

Now, the next few moments would probably have been confusing even with the benefit of subtitles and instant video replay, but add to that a pinch of shock and panic, and Rogers' notoriously slippy memory when it came to names, and you have a recipe for two minutes of pure chaos. Rogers got the ball rolling:

"Jack!"

"Edward," replied Nugent with a weary sigh.

"No, I'm Peter."

"No, I know you are. I mean I'm Edward, Peter. Even though you sometimes called me Jack."

"Do I?"

"Yes. You just did. It doesn't matter. Call me Jack if it helps."

"What would help me most right now, Jack, is knowing why you are standing in my lounge wearing a frock and a furry hat."

"I can explain everything," spluttered Nugent.

"Start with the frock," insisted Rogers.

119

"All right. It's a long story."

"That's fine. I'm retired."

Nugent started pacing the room, a sure sign that he was about to cut a short story long. "Well, do you remember Edward?"

"But you said that you were Edward!" Rogers was doing his best to keep up, but it wasn't easy to accept such apparently contradictory information from someone whose gender was still up for grabs.

"We're both Edward," snapped Nugent, who was now barely able to hide his mounting frustration. "Surely you must remember Edward Jones? The man you sent to see me. The man with the bald patch that went away."

Rogers' eyes suddenly lit up. "Oh, yes, of course! With the Polaroid. That's why I know your face. But...last time I saw you, you were a man. In fact, you both were."

"We both still are," replied Edward patiently. "We're in disguise."

"Not, if I may venture an opinion, a very convincing one," retorted Roger indignantly.

"Look, Peter, we haven't got time to mess around, we need..." Nugent stopped. He thought he'd seen something. A shadow moving in the hall. He brought his finger to his lips with all the drama of a Samurai swordsman brandishing his ceremonial weapon, and the room fell deadly silent. A floorboard creaked. Three pairs of eyes widened.

Someone was listening behind the door.

The Samurai swordsman pounced. It all happened in a blur. The intruder was dragged screaming into the lounge, and fifteen stones of bald, cross-dressing Yorkshireman tossed him brusquely to the floor and straddled his shoulders.

"All right, you bastard - who do you work for?" screamed Nugent.

A muffled reply.

"Lift your frock up, Ted. Let's see his face," suggested Edward.

"Oh. Right."

It's hard to know who was most traumatized - Rogers, on seeing his new friend squashed under his old friend, or Sarah, who had just spent twelve long seconds with her head up a sweaty man's skirt.

Rogers attempted to come to the rescue, claiming it was just his new friend Suzie Appletree. But Nugent, paranoid about undercover paparazzi, needed more convincing.

"Suzie Appletree, eh? Is that your real name?"

Nugent could be an intimidating figure when roused, and roused he most certainly was, so Sarah thought she'd better play it straight. "Er, well, no. My real name is Sarah Appleby."

"Aha!" bellowed Nugent triumphantly. "So you are undercover!"

"I was, until you lifted your skirt."

Edward thought he'd better do his bit for clarity, so he chipped in with a far more straightforward question. "Are you, or are you not, a reporter?"

"Not. Who the hell are you?"

"Don't tell her, Edward." screamed Nugent.

"So your name's Edward," deduced Sarah.

"Oh, thanks, Ted," snorted Edward.

"And your name's Ted."

"Oh, brilliant!" exploded Nugent. "She's blown our cover."

Sarah's frustration finally boiled over. "What cover? What the hell are you doing here?"

The next twenty seconds were devoted entirely to a four-way row, during which everyone shouted and no-one heard a word. But it was Sarah's dog Jack who added the finishing touch to the chaos. He bounded in and, assuming his master was being attacked (which wasn't a bad assumption) the canine wasted no time in sinking his canines deep into the aggressor's bottom and clamping his jaws tightly together. The idea, so far as we can see into the beast's mind, was presumably to extract maximum discomfort levels for the aggressor, thereby causing him to desist in his harassment of the master. If so, it worked a treat.

Nugent screamed, jumped up and wheeled round in pain, spinning the attached invisible canine around like an unorthodox hammer-thrower, and in the process clearing the mantelpiece of all its ceramic collectibles. Understandably, this left at least two people in the room assuming that Nugent had gone, dare I use the pun, completely barking mad. They could hear dog-like noises, of course, but they coincided perfectly with Nugent's own gritted teeth yelps and howls, so the inescapable conclusion was that the poor man was in the grip of some kind of werewolf moment.

Sarah, of course, knew the root cause of Nugent's discomfort, and once he had stopped flailing his arms and legs around like a demented whirling dervish, he crash-landed inelegantly face-down on the floor, allowing Sarah to calmly move in and detach her spaniel from his bottom. This she did with the consummate ease that only comes from years of practice, pressing on exactly the right spot to make his jaws spring open.

"It's all right, Jack. I'm okay," said Sarah, now apparently talking to her own arms. "How did you get out of your collar, eh? Excuse me."

Sarah exited momentarily, and returned with Jack in his collar. Or, if you prefer the action from the point of view of the others in the room, she returned with a floating dog collar.

Nugent, Rogers and Edward, meanwhile, watched open-mouthed and silent. There was an awkward pause. In fact, no - I take it back - to call it an awkward pause is a little unfair on your average awkward pause, which typically covers situations like the vicar innocently asking you and your wife at the Church bazaar why the flirty new dance teacher's blue Toyota was parked on your drive for two hours last Wednesday evening - the night of your wife's new flower arranging course.

This particular pause was not so much awkward as totally out of control, and Sarah sensed that the pressure to provide some sort of vaguely plausible explanation had now become irresistible. She gave a small, dry cough, and proceeded.

"Okay, so I have an invisible dog."

Sarah thought the explanation went pretty well, but even she didn't expect to get away without at least one follow-up question. Edward was the first to take up the challenge.

"You have a what?"

"An invisible dog."

"Oh, that's all right then. For a moment there I thought something weird was going on here."

Rogers tried to sketch in a little more detail. "Are you trying to tell us, my dear, that your dog is… well…invisible?"

"That's exactly what I did tell you."

"I see."

"No you don't. Well, not the dog, anyway."

"Forgive my cynicism," replied the genial old doctor, "but I'm not really a great one for the supernatural. I confess I'm not entirely clear what your motivation could be for playing this little practical joke, my dear, but I think that in all likelihood what we are looking at here is simply one of those trick dog collars you can buy in a joke shop."

Nugent was still in shock, but nevertheless more than capable of contributing to the debate. "Trick dog collars, Peter, do not bite you on the arse."

"I'm sorry about that," replied Sarah. "He thought you were attacking me."

To be fair, the mysterious mutt did have a point. In fact, he had several, all razor sharp. Nugent, who had been squeezing both hands firmly on his buttocks to help numb the pain, suddenly decided he needed to retrieve one of them to wipe the sweat from his brow. And that was when he spotted a considerable amount of red liquid smeared on his palm.

"Oh, my God - blood!"

"Oh, terrific," said Edward. "Here we go again."

And here indeed we did go again, as Nugent went spark out and proceeded to bleed profusely all over the white sheepskin hearth rug.

Now even though this latest development was distressing for Rogers, who was rather fond of his rug, and also for Nugent, who was rather fond of staying conscious, it actually turned out to be a handy distraction for Sarah, who at least for a while avoided having to face any more awkward questions about translucent spaniels.

Much shouting ensued, as frantic attempts were made to return both man and rug to their former glories. Edward and Sarah took it in turns to slap Nugent repeatedly, while Rogers was busy ferrying bucketfuls of water from the kitchen to the lounge in the vain hope of at least diluting the damage. Nugent ignored several shrieked instructions along the lines of "Wake up!", "Roll off the rug!" and the somewhat harsh "Stop bleeding!" and continued doing a passable impersonation of a badly-injured and beached whale.

He was, however, eventually revived when a bucketful of cold water destined for the rug accidentally hit him full in the face. That's when things reached a natural crescendo. Shocked out of his slumbers, a bewildered Nugent proceeded to add his own considerable vocal energy to the ensemble. In fact, it was hard to imagine how four people could have made more noise without the aid of a drum kit and the Glastonbury public address system, so it was even more surprising when a fifth member of the band suddenly stepped on to stage, cranked up the volume, and let rip with a blistering solo.

"Beeeeeeeeeeeeee quiet!" bellowed the voice of a ridiculously posh old lady. And what a voice. It was simply massive. Somewhere in that tiny frame she must have her own built-in woofers, tweeters and bass bins. The instruction rumbled through the floorboards, it zinged through the air, it pounded on the chest cavity. All four protagonists and the clandestine canine instantly obeyed. There was no choice. The room fell eerily silent.

They turned their heads slowly towards the strange, wrinkled chrysalis lying by the door. Mrs Rogers had wriggled and hopped her way down the stairs to see what all the commotion was. Visually, she was an intimidating and surreal figure. But, above all, it was that voice. They were fully expecting her next words to be "Fee, Fi, Fo, Fum." They were close.

"What on earth is going on here?" she barked, with all the fire and authority of an ex public school headmistress and practising magistrate, which she was.

"Erm...allow me to introduce my wife," said Rogers.

*   *   *

The next fifteen minutes were far too complex to transcribe, but suffice it to say that, by the end of it, everyone had at least an inkling of who was who, and possessed a rudimentary understanding of why a room that contained three men, two women and a dog, actually looked more like a room containing three women, one man, no dog and a rather large chrysalis.

Formal introductions over, the negotiating parties prepared to move into the slightly trickier second phase, explaining the nub of Edward's predicament and what he was doing there. That's not to say that the small matter of Sarah's peep-through pooch had been entirely shelved. That was under the category unfinished business, and was bound to pop up on the agenda again sooner or later.

There was a short interval for running repairs (Nugent's bottom desperately needed a bandage and Muriel's legs didn't, so they did a deal) and then Sarah took centre stage. Actually, there wasn't a stage as such, but there was the next best thing, a rather damp, camp, pink hearthrug.

She took it from the top - exploding grannies, fruit flies et al - and it was a virtuoso performance. Sarah held her audience, aptly enough for a witch in full flow, spellbound for over an hour.

"But why fruit flies?" asked Edward, when she finally opened up the session to questions from the floor.

"Well, it's no good doing tests on something like a dog, or a cat, because it lives too long. You'd have to wait around years to see if the experiment has had any effect. But fruit flies have such a short natural lifespan that they're ideal for testing different methodologies to see which gives the best results."

"Sound scientific principles," chipped in Rogers, with a sort of 'That's my girl!' pride. He, of course, had heard some of the fruit fly story from Sarah the evening before over a drink or six, but was heartily enjoying the reprise.

"Thank you," continued Sarah, who was now secretly beginning to enjoy the limelight. "My early experiments were really promising. I'd managed to get them to live to the human equivalent of about five hundred years old."

"Good Lord," exclaimed Rogers, who hadn't heard this particular fact before, or if he had, he'd quickly forgotten it under the influence of a whisky anaesthetic. "Five hundred years, eh? And what exactly is that, my dear?"

"About a month," replied Sarah.

"Oh." Rogers did his best not to look deflated. "Still impressive though."

"The pharmaceutical companies started pushing to do human trials. And then…"

"And then what?" quizzed the chrysalis.

"And then, one day, without warning, one of the fruit flies suddenly swelled up to the size of a tennis ball and…well, exploded - into a mist of yellow sticky vapour."

"Good Lord!" said Rogers again, this time with enough extra emphasis to merit an exclamation mark and a raised eyebrow. "Dead?"

"Er…yes. Very much so. Closely followed by all the rest. They just kept swelling up and, well, popping off. Something had made them become unstable."

"But what?" Rogers enquired, the eyebrow still a good inch above its natural resting position.

Sarah shrugged her shoulders. "Who knows? I couldn't really do a post-mortem. The human trials were postponed."

"Oh, shame," Edward contributed drily.

"I didn't give up, of course. First I made some radical adjustments to the food formula."

"And?" prompted Rogers, the wayward eyebrow now coming in to land.

"And my dog became invisible."

The eyebrow aborted the landing and headed sharply back upwards, where it was joined in formation by its colleague.

"Don't ask me how," continued Sarah, just before someone had the chance to ask her how, "I've never been able to repeat the conditions. All I know is that Jack scoffed all the banana extract and just, well…vanished."

Edward, who had been quick to spot the potential of a cure for baldness, was now instantly taken with the idea that Sarah may have accidentally stumbled on a potion which could finally help him fulfil his greatest childhood fantasy. Ever since he'd first read about the Invisible Man in his Marvel comics, his rampant teenage hormones had gone into overdrive, imagining what it would be like to sneak into the houses of beautiful women and watch them taking a shower. While other young men dreamt of having supernatural strength, saving the planet and foiling Lex Luthor, or out-witting the Riddler with a fascinating beltful of bat-gadgets, or running up skyscrapers effortlessly like a human spider, he'd never quite seen the point of such childish nonsense, preferring instead to spend many a distracted afternoon standing in Raquel Welch's boudoir, watching her prepare for bed. This was only possible for the Invisible Man, of course, if he too was totally naked, a thought which added extra zest to the fantasy. Of course, Edward had long since buried all such silly adolescent ambitions under several crusted layers of boring maturity. But that's not to say they couldn't be resurrected. After all, some men reach forty and suddenly decide to buy a motorbike, or get a tattoo. Perhaps he should treat himself.

"So, this banana extract. What happens if humans eat it?" asked Edward, with a squeaky, nervous air badly disguised as nonchalance.

"It just makes them fat - trust me," replied Sarah, bringing Edward's mental ramble to a swift and disappointing end. "So then I tried something else. I increased the strength of the magnetic field, reversed the polarity, and applied a strong but intermittent static charge."

Rogers circled and tried again. "And?"

"And my house exploded."

Both eyebrows went off the radar.

"That's fascinating. What do you make of it, Jack - you haven't said much yet?"

Even though his name wasn't Jack, Ted Nugent knew his time had come. He thanked Sarah for her candid revelations, and took his place on the pink podium, formerly known as Rogers' hearthrug. He proceeded to explain the trying circumstances that had led him to Rogers' house. He saw no point in holding back on the facts, as the world's press had already let the cat and a whole litter of kittens out of the bag, so he prepared to explain all to his attentive audience.

It wasn't an easy assignment. Such a story took some selling even at the best of times, but try doing it dressed in a frock and furry hat. Credibility is stretched to breaking point. However, he couldn't have wished for a better warm-up act than Sarah's invisible dog story, so he felt confident that the audience was well and truly softened up and ready for more tales of the unexpected.

"It's even more fascinating than you realize, Peter," Nugent began earnestly. "You see, I too have experimented with static charges. Have I not, Edward?"

"Yes," said Edward, who had never been one to waffle. Besides, he was still sulking about the lost Invisible Man opportunity.

It was time for Sarah's eyebrows to make their own modest gesture - a little quiver followed by a three and a half degree clockwise shift from the horizontal. "Why?"

Nugent proceeded with relish. "I devised a particularly complex test involving a series of small static charges being sent through Edward's body to try and mimic the effect of lightning. You see, Edward also has a little secret, don't you, Edward?"

"Hardly a secret any more," replied Edward.

"Well, do come on!" enthused Rogers. "We're all intrigued."

"Edward Jones was struck by lightning, five years ago. As you can see, ladies and gentlemen, he survived. More than survived, actually. Ever since then, he's been, well... how can I put this?"

"Straightforwardly," suggested Edward, who was still bearing the mental and physical scars of Nugent's earlier attempt to break the facts to him gently.

Nugent took the hint. "He's been getting younger. His whole metabolism has gone into reverse."

Now, that's not the sort of statement you make every day, so it was interesting to note the different reactions. The elderly Rogers was dumbfounded, which is pretty much what you'd expect, and his eyebrows needed oxygen. His wife, too, was quite clearly taken aback. It took a lot more than this, of course, to actually soften her upper lip, but on hearing this startling news there was a definite twitch and, had the correct type of industrial sensors been fitted, the early signs of a subtle stress fracture might have been detected.

But Sarah, now, that was weird. No look of surprise, no questioning of the facts - just a private, enigmatic smile. Edward was quick to notice her reaction, or rather lack of it.

"Did you hear what he said?"

"Yes."

"I'm getting younger."

"Yes."

"Instead of older."

"Yes."

"That sort of makes me...unique, in a sort of earth-shatteringly unique never before on this planet sort of way."

"Yes. Yes it does."

"Have you always been this excitable?"

Sarah's smile gently broadened, and she fixed Edward with a seductively magnetic stare. "I knew you'd come." Her huge brown eyes twinkled mischievously, and Edward felt his insides tingle.

"What do you mean?" he croaked.

Now, whether or not Sarah would have been forthcoming with an explanation at that point we'll never know, because suddenly, after a long period of uncharacteristic silence, the chrysalis intervened.

"I've never heard such a load of poppycock in all my life," she boomed. Clearly, the upper lip which just a few moments ago had been showing signs of distress had been in for emergency repairs. A few spot welds later it was back on duty, stronger than ever. "Getting younger indeed. Stuff and nonsense. Total balderdash. Utter rot and twaddle. Where's your proof?"

It's not that Muriel was the sort that closed her mind to the dark recesses of the supernatural and all things spooky - far from it. After all, she seemed to embrace the whole invisible dog scenario as calmly as you like. But that was mainly because she could see the dog with her own eyes, or not, if you know what I mean. Muriel, who'd spent many a distinguished hour laying down the law from behind a magistrate's bench, had trained her mind over many years to ignore the vagaries of hearsay, rumour and supposition, and to form judgments based only on the facts before her. In short, proof is what she required, and evidence of the invisible spaniel, if not the beast itself, was there for all to see, or in Nugent's case, to feel. But when it came to the main item on the agenda, namely Edward's potential regression to childhood, Muriel for one was all ready to call the police and warn them to have a brace of strait-jackets in their armoury, for she was convinced that Nugent and his trouser-suited friend were nothing short of a couple of delirious fruitcakes.

Luckily, though, the cynics were out-numbered by the believers.

Rogers, even if he could never quite remember Nugent's name, was more than familiar with the brilliance of his mind. They had, after all, been at University together - they'd shared a flat, shared grand ideas - even at one point shared a girlfriend - and Rogers knew that if it hadn't been for Nugent's obsessive quest to cure his own premature baldness, he would undoubtedly have gone on to become one of the century's great scientific minds, eventually freeing the world of some dread disease and featuring on the back of a ten pound note.

What's more, of course, Rogers had witnessed the phenomenon of Edward Jones' reversible bald patch with his own eyes - he'd even photographed it. So if Jack Nugent, or Ted, or whatever his best friend's name actually was, claimed that Edward was getting younger, then that was good enough for him. He didn't understand it, but he was definitely on board.

That's one for, one against. The dog abstained, so it was down to Sarah Appleby to give the casting vote. And it was Sarah who was most entranced by this remarkable tale. After all, her own scientific career had been entirely devoted to the holy grail of prolonging life beyond the norm, and here before her was a man who'd apparently cracked it without even trying, and in an entirely novel way.

So, Sarah it was who devoured the story with maximum relish, and she kept pushing for more and more detail. She wanted to know everything Edward could remember about the day he was struck by lightning, what he'd eaten and whether it involved bananas. She also wanted to know every little nuance of the tests Nugent had performed, how the results had been interpreted, and why - all the time mentally cross-checking the data with her own fruit fly experiments and searching for any potential correlations.

She was particularly interested in the fact that Edward worked near electricity pylons, which opened up an intense new debate about the mysterious and virtually uncharted influence of electro-magnetic fields on the human condition.

Edward Jones, Mr Rogers, his wife Muriel and Jack the see-through spaniel sat back in awe as the two scientists became completely engrossed in their intense technical exchanges.

It became clear that, despite having an undeniable edge of eccentricity, Sarah was well on top of her subject, and easily a match for Nugent's brilliant mind. For the next two hours, the two boffins swapped ideas and theories like two excited kids swapping whatever it is that kids get excited about swapping these days - Ninja cards, obscure plastic blobs, Charlie Chan stickers and the like. But it was only when Nugent mentioned that he had recently performed one final test on Edward - a particularly complex experiment involving a series of small static charges being sent through his body to try and mimic the effect of lightning - that Sarah's enthusiasm moved up a gear from the merely ecstatic to the positively orgasmic.

What sent Sarah's pulse racing was the fact that she herself had once put a great deal of store in the whole electric shock theory. Indeed, quite early on in her quest for the immortal truth, she'd performed a very similar series of experiments on her fruit flies. For Sarah, unfortunately, the data had proved disappointing, in that every fly she tested died instantly. This, from a scientific point of view, made it much harder to determine how much its life might have been extended had it lived. In the end, she reluctantly dropped the theory and moved on to exploring the power of magnetic fields, much to the relief of the fly next in line, who'd heard stories of how his friends had gone off to work for the Government and never returned.

But learning that Edward Jones, the human fruit fly, had not only survived the test but also seemed to be thriving on it, was enough to rekindle Sarah's enthusiasm. In fact, rekindle is too mild a word. The effect was rather more like that of pouring petrol onto a bonfire. Sarah exploded with energy, jabbering excitedly to Nugent and Edward about her original theories on electrical therapy, and how she felt convinced that it would have ultimately extended the life of her fruit flies, had it not killed them first.

The Rogers' household had never seen so much activity. As night fell, three men, two women and an invisible dog sat exhausted, exhilarated and confused.

Meanwhile, outside, the world anxiously waited for news of Edward Jones.

CHAPTER THIRTEEN

When the modern media get their teeth into a big story, nothing short of an even bigger story can make them let go. But, quite simply, there was no bigger story than this, nor was there ever likely to be.

Overnight, Ted Nugent's stolen lab notes had mysteriously made their way into the clutches of a tabloid editor. They seemed to put to rest any lingering suspicions that this might be an elaborate hoax - after all, when a story appears on the front page of a tabloid, it must be true - and by the next day Edward Jones was seriously hot property.

As the story broke, the Jones' household was immediately put under tight twenty-four hour police supervision, but reporters on the scent of a major exclusive are a resourceful bunch. One of the paparazzi was arrested because, even though he was not technically standing on Edward Jones' property, the tip of his seventeen foot long camera lens was actually inside the porch. Ingeniously, the considerable weight of the lens was supported by a piece of string attached to a large helium balloon, which caused the police to check the legal niceties with a local judge to see if they had any jurisdiction over the airspace above the house.

But the prize for creative endeavour went to two television reporters who were arrested for trying to tunnel under the garden to gain access to the lounge. They were only discovered when a sharp-eyed bobby spotted dirt coming from the bottom of the trousers of one the reporters as he paraded up and down the road. After intensive interrogation of the 'dirt man', as he became known, the police raided a neighbour's garden shed, and found his accomplice hidden inside a wooden-lined shaft under an old stove.

Inside the house, Mary and Martin Jones were being interviewed by the man heading up the investigation, Detective Inspector Alan Thompson. As he made clear to them, Edward didn't appear to have broken any laws (the police were yet to learn of his involvement with the stolen car) but his disappearance was fast becoming a major public order issue, so if they did know anything about his whereabouts it was best to own up now.

Martin said he couldn't own up, because he didn't know anything, except what he'd read in the papers. Mary just cried a lot. DI Thompson had just had a similar story from the Nugent household, where a distraught Mrs Nugent had given no clues whatsoever as to where her husband might be, but did through a flood of tears report a missing frock and furry hat.

It was now Saturday morning, and Edward Jones and Dr Nugent had been missing for twenty-four hours. According to police guidelines, this didn't yet officially make them missing persons, merely persons who were missing, but nevertheless they were nowhere to be found.

DI Thompson decided that he wouldn't get any sense out of Mary until she stopped crying, and probably not even then, so when dutiful son Martin said he'd finally had enough and was going down the pub, Thompson cut his losses and went with him.

If deserting Mary in such trying circumstances seems a little ungallant, well, you really just had to be there. Mary didn't just cry, she wailed and shrieked, and she did it in a manner which would tempt even the most mild-mannered and devout pacifist, fresh from an inspiring course on political correctness, to give her a good slapping.

Not that Mary was alone for long. No sooner had the front door clicked shut than the back door burst open. It was her sister, Glenda.

Now, if you had to make a prioritized list of all the people you don't want stomping up your stairs at that precise moment, Glenda would probably just be pipped into second place, immediately behind the Grim Reaper. Glenda, in a word, was scary.

If you thought that ugly sisters only existed in pantomimes, think again. She looked like a 1960's Bulgarian shot putter, but without any of the elegance - or, for those of you old enough to remember this, the woman who used to play the SPECTRE assassin in early Bond movies, with a flick-knife hidden in her shoe and hair that looked as if it had been cut by an Eastern Block council contractor who held a grudge. This, of course, was before the seventies, when suddenly all female Bond villains became super glamorous lithe sex vixens with exotic names like Clitia, who managed to do all of their spying in black lycra cat-suits. The suits usually had a handy front zip and concealed all manner of clever gadgets - my favourite was a set of gravity-defying breasts.

A random hormone test on Glenda would probably have revealed that biologically she lay somewhere between male and bovine. But, despite almost being one herself, her views on men were decidedly vicious, and when it came to handing out relationship advice, Glenda didn't take any prisoners.

Her mission today was a simple one, to comfort her sister by reminding her that all men were scum, and that she should have taken her initial advice and never married Edward, or anyone else, in the first place. This was extremely reassuring for Mary, whose condition rapidly deteriorated from wailing wife to half-crazed banshee.

Glenda, however, wasted no time in giving her sister the good slapping she was clearly asking for, and she soon had her total attention.

"He's no good for you, Mary - never has been,

never will be."

"But…"

"If you've got any sense you'll divorce him now, before he makes you the laughing-stock of the whole village."

"But…"

"He's just using you, Mary. That's all men ever do. They use you. To make their sandwiches. Then they throw you on the scrap heap."

Quite where Glenda had received all this worldly wisdom it was hard to say. It certainly wasn't from first-hand experience. She'd never been married herself, mainly because she'd never had anything that might remotely be termed a boyfriend. In fact, the nearest she'd ever got to being dated was when she once stood too near to a cage at Dudley Zoo, and the resident gorilla made a grab for her blouse. It turned out, though, that the gorilla was only after her picnic box, so in a sense he too was only using her to make his sandwiches.

Glenda's tirade against Edward was, at this point, based purely on what she'd read in the newspaper, and as far as she was concerned it was all a load of drivel. The basic facts were clear enough. Mary's husband had deserted her. He'd run away - possibly with another woman, but probably with another man, this Nugent chap.

Thus far, Glenda had been content to condemn Edward without a single shred of evidence, but when Mary then let it slip that her husband had actually been wearing her red trouser suit, well, this was like red rag to a bull, almost literally.

"Hah! There you go, then! He's a transvestite! I knew it. Most of them are."

Quite what this meant we're not sure. But it was enough to upset Mary's delicate equilibrium, and she once again dissolved into a dramatic squeal of anguish, inadvertently splitting the ear drums of a TV journalist who'd just that second managed to point a sensitive directional microphone towards the bedroom window, cranked up the amplifier to maximum, and donned his headphones.

As a screaming, delirious Mary began repeatedly pummelling the bedroom floor with her feet and fists, Glenda knew her work was done. Another convert. Another female who had lost faith in the male of the species once and for all. Revenge is sweet.

Smug in victory, Glenda emerged from the front door and pushed her way through the paparazzi who, curiously, after an initial flurry of activity to point and focus their lenses, slowly withdrew their eyes from the viewfinders and decided not to take any photographs. She'd left behind a sister who could best be described as emotionally sabotaged. Mary had never been particularly strong-willed, and Glenda had got inside her head as easily as she'd got inside her back door. She had a key for both. And the key to Mary Jones' mind was a deep-seated fear of scandal.

Embarrassment, in any shape or form, was Mary's Achilles heel. Even though she'd hardly ever spoken to her neighbours over the years, what they were presumed to think of her had shaped much of Mary's life. It dictated when she drew the curtains, when she switched off the lights, how many empty wine bottles were left by the dustbin, the time she hoovered, the frequency with which she hoovered, the clothing that was hung on the washing line, how often she creosoted the fence or cut the lawn - even the time she went to bed. It was one of the aspects of her personality that had driven Edward to distraction, along with all the other aspects of her personality.

But she couldn't help it. It was how she'd been brought up. Her parents, now sadly both deceased, might just as well have been Victoria and Albert. You can imagine, then, how hard the events of the last twenty-four hours had hit her. With the media crawling all over the Jones' household like ants on strawberry jam, the unbearable thought of facing the whispering neighbours (not to mention the whole country) and the immediate influence of her sister's brutal but wholly plausible pep talk, Mary Jones was left feeling that she now had only two honourable exit routes available to her - immediate divorce, or pushing a ceremonial sword through her ribcage.

Not having any ceremonial swords to hand, she reluctantly decided that perhaps her sister was right, and that it may be time to start a new life without Edward. Whatever he'd done or not done, it was clear that he'd done it without confiding in her, which was hurtful enough in itself. But it was also clear that he was going to be a focal point for the gossips and the media for many months and years to come, and it was a life that she simply couldn't bear to contemplate. She had become, as Glenda had so cruelly and deliberately pointed out, the laughing-stock of the village.

She desperately wanted to talk it through with the only other directly affected party - her son, Martin. Unfortunately, when he arrived home from the pub three hours later, his image as the innocent emotional victim whose feelings urgently needed to be considered was somewhat compromised by the fact that he'd had eleven pints.

As a result, his response to Mary's trembling, tearful question "Martin, darling, how would you feel if your father and I got a divorce?" was hardly likely to tug on any heart strings.

"Do what you fucking like," he barked, at which point he farted loudly and collapsed on the settee.

Martin was always considered to be the successful element of the Jones' marriage, the bright spot on an otherwise misty horizon, so in that split second Mary's upset turned to anger and resolve. She grabbed her coat, and stormed defiantly out of the house and through the crowds. The street scene crackled into life - cameras flashing, microphones thrusting, agitated reporters shouting and jostling for position.

"Mrs Jones!" called one of the throng through the melee. "Can you tell us where your husband is?"

The question went straight to the heart of Mary's torment, mainly because she didn't know the answer. She turned, and proudly flicked back her head. "I have no husband!" she proclaimed, and then immediately jumped straight onto the number 38 bus.

As the bus passed Tesco and rounded the corner towards the town centre, Mary was still in a tearful daze. Divorce? It was such a huge step - indeed it was the first time in years that she'd taken an active interest in her husband - but the words of her sister were still ringing deliriously in her ears:

"If you've got any sense you'll divorce him now, before he makes you the laughing-stock of the whole village," screamed Glenda, her huge face distorted through a grotesque fish-eye lens which dominated the landscape of Mary's imagination. The last few syllables then kept echoing over and over in her head - each repeat getting louder and more distorted, the face growing and twisting:

"laughing-stock...**laughing stock... LAUGHING STOCK...STOCK...TOCK...OCK!!**"

She came out of her day-mare with a start, beads of cold sweat breaking out all over her brow.

"Last stop, lady," droned the driver wearily.

Mary stepped off the bus, reluctantly accepting that legal separation from Edward now seemed to offer the only dignified way out of her dilemma.

Besides, she'd just told the world's press that she had no husband, and some of the neighbours had probably heard her say it, so there was no going back.

She wasn't sure how exactly one went about filing for divorce, so she asked at the Post Office, assuming they'd have a form for it. They hadn't, but Mrs Perkins behind the counter was extremely helpful, and suggested that she talked to Crabtree, Crabtree & Whippet, the solicitors who'd recently handled her divorce. They'd apparently done a really nice job for the money, and she was now recommending them to all her friends, even if they were happily married.

Forgive the slight diversion here, but if you're in any way interested in the mechanics of business, or fancy yourself as a bit of an entrepreneur, or simply want a few pointers about making a success of the family firm, you could do far worse than to study the techniques of Messrs Crabtree, Crabtree & Whippet. Incidentally, if this sort of thing bores you, by all means skip the next few paragraphs and there'll be no hard feelings. But don't blame me if your company fails as a direct result.

Crabtree, Crabtree & Whippet, ironically known as 'The Family Solicitors', had over the last few years carved quite a lucrative little niche market for themselves by specializing in divorces. Their marketing strategy was simple, but inspired. They acquired a database of the names and addresses of newly-weds from the local Church and Registry

Office, and then wrote to every couple at twelve month intervals, offering a money-off voucher should they decide to untie the knot.

It worked a treat. Over one-third of their letters eventually came up trumps, putting the two percent industry standard success rate for direct mail totally to shame. And off the back of the divorces they also did a roaring trade in the drawing up of lease agreements for rented properties - usually two per couple.

But not content to let market forces dictate the pace of change, CC&W pro-actively managed the business pipeline. They would target wealthy male prospects, follow them around in disguise, and systematically scupper their chances of marital bliss with a series of ingenious teaser campaigns. There was the surreptitious squirt of perfume on the back of the neck, the bra stuffed under the car seat, the casual planting of condoms in the jacket pocket.

Such discoveries by the female of the species inevitably took their toll, and it was only a matter of time before a representative of CC&W would be shaking the hand of their victim's spouse in the office: "Mrs Jenkins - what can I do for you?"

At one time it was even rumoured that, when business was slack, they would send out batches of scented letters from an anonymous lover to every male on the database, but nothing was ever proven.

Very occasionally, however, the dubious working practices of Crabtree, Crabtree & Whippet might backfire, such as the time Mr Whippet's supply of plantable condoms was found in his pocket by Mrs Whippet, who then promptly kicked him into touch. But even then, the divorce was handled by Mr Crabtree, so Whippet indirectly benefited from the additional profits.

All in all, CC&W had made a remarkable success from the failure and misery of others, and they could be rightly proud of their achievements. But their ingenuity didn't end there.

Young Mr James Crabtree, great-grandson of one of the original partners, had recently brought the firm smartly into the twenty-first century by launching the country's first e-divorce website. The site featured some truly cutting-edge solutions to separation. Once it had collected your credit card details, all you did was point and click to get the solution that was right for you.

The menu system guided you through some basic principles. For example, on the male home page there was a drop-down box allowing you to choose between "Amicable settlement", "Tough and business-like" or "Crucify the bitch" - and there was even a handy online calculator which could automatically work out how much money you'd have left when the dust had settled.

The website was a great hit with busy, modern couples who simply hadn't got time to get into town, and who demanded the convenience of being able to track their day-to-day marital status online.

The site also featured a link to an online lonely hearts dating agency called 'Second Time Lucky', which offered a discount to CC&W customers. A quick check with Companies House revealed the three directors of 'Second Time Lucky' to be none other than a Mr Crabtree, a Mr Crabtree, and a Mr Whippet.

The dating agency did a roaring trade from the divorcees, and in turn the divorce business eventually inherited customers back from the dating agency. Many of the regulars had been on the books for years - some were on their third or fourth divorce with CC&W, spawning the satellite companies 'Third Time Lucky' and 'Fourth Time Lucky'. It was a truly loyal customer base, who wouldn't dream of going anywhere else for their failed marriages.

Forgive me, I did rather get side-tracked by Messrs Crabtree, Crabtree & Whippet, but given how much a typical modern business spends on sales training, trendy marketing strategies, people development, in-sourcing, out-sourcing, sales gurus and all the other commercial paraphernalia, I'm tempted to develop the last few paragraphs into a management handbook with accompanying video.

Where was I? Oh, yes. Mary Jones.

There, between the butcher's and Help the Aged was a doorway, just as Mrs Perkins had said, and on the wall by the door, an old, tarnished brass plaque.

'Crabtree, Crabtree & Whippet, Family Solicitors' it said. And underneath, with no attempt to match the colouration, size, style or typeface of the original sign, a new strip of brass had been added, proudly bearing the italicized tag line: 'Your divorce is our business'.

Mary, anxiously checking over her shoulder to see if anyone was looking, tried peering through the glass pane, but it was too dark inside to make anything out, so she tentatively pushed open the door.

Once inside, she found herself faced by a narrow set of steep stairs leading, presumably, to the offices above the shops. At the top of the stairs, barely making an impression through the gloom, was a single, dreary, low-wattage light bulb, guarded by a restless moth, which was busy casting gigantic shadows on the dirty magnolia walls.

Inside the doorway, abandoned on the lino floor, lay dozens of envelopes marked 'Return to sender' and 'Not known at this address'. They were stamped not only by the post office, but also by the muddy footprints of countless visitors.

Somewhere between the butcher's and Help the Aged - it might just have been a metaphorical as well as a literal description of the solicitors' whereabouts. Mary lost her nerve and turned to go.

"Aargh!"

She jumped out of her skin. A greasy-looking man in a greasy-looking suit had somehow greased in behind her, and now offered a greasy smile.

"You must be Mary!" he greased, holding out his greasy hand. "James Crabtree! Mrs Perkins at the post office said you'd be here. Shall we go up to my office?"

CHAPTER FOURTEEN

Meanwhile, in the wider world, the story was breaking in the most spectacular fashion. Not surprisingly, news that it might be possible to reach forty and then start growing younger was going down pretty big in the States. Suddenly, Botox and liposuction were so yesterday. A new and more extreme version of cosmetic surgery, already dubbed 'pyloning', was hitting the headlines.

In the Beverly Hills area alone, the police reported hundreds of cases of huge-breasted women with distended lips strapping themselves to electricity pylons and praying for an electrical storm. This was a dangerous game - especially if you got what you wished for - and one unfortunate lady, quite literally, had her tits blown off. She was found to be dead on arrival at hospital. Worse still, she was back to a 32B. One of her implants had partially melted onto a cow below, who now proudly wears it like a bobble hat.

In Japan, a businessman with terminal bad taste had reportedly offered a $500 million reward for the first person to find Edward and successfully extract his DNA. Meanwhile, religious leaders were running around like headless chickens, desperately trying to put whatever spin they could on the raw data to make it all sound like part of the boss's master plan.

From headless chickens, to headless topiary peacocks. Edward Jones, Dr Nugent, Mr and Mrs Rogers, Sarah Appleby and Jack the perspicacious puppy sat watching the TV reports in awe.

In the face of all the new evidence now presented before her, Muriel Rogers had long since conceded that her transvestite guests were not mad after all, and that something very special was taking place in her lounge. All of them, in fact, without having to express anything formally, had realized that they were becoming uniquely bonded. In pure news terms, they were now the centre of the known universe. Everyone wanted to share their secret, and that, instinctively, made them determined that no-one else would.

For Edward Jones, though, it was all getting a bit much. He hadn't slept properly for what seemed like weeks (but was actually just a week) and he was starting to look dreadful. Getting younger was putting years on him. He was tired. Dog tired. In fact, he was even more tired than the dog, who didn't look tired at all - or if he did, he wasn't showing it. And no wonder. For the last few days in particular, Edward Jones had been surviving on a diet of pure adrenalin.

Adrenalin, of course, is pretty useful stuff when delivered in small doses. It sharpens the senses, speeds the reactions, and can help get you out of a tight spot if, for example, you're being chased by a bear. But let's be honest - being chased by a bear isn't, for your average British citizen, an everyday occurrence. This is exactly as nature intended, and consequently adrenalin was only ever designed to be delivered to the body in short and infrequent squirts. Edward, unfortunately, was binge-drinking the stuff, having it delivered daily in large barrels stacked on dray carts. This inevitably was putting undue strain on the small gland tasked with producing the magic liquid, and it would only be a matter of time before something gave out.

And he wasn't the only one feeling the strain. Nugent was also a man under enormous pressure. Sadly, he'd never been in the rudest of health. One of the first things he learnt as a young student doctor was the terrible damage that alcohol can do to your liver. This invaluable knowledge came not from dry lectures or text books, but from drinking outrageous amounts of alcohol on a nightly basis. Worried that he might eventually become an alcoholic, he turned to drink.

Only Ted Nugent's even greater obsession with finding a cure for his own baldness kept him from the gutter. At one point, he had to face up to the nightmare scenario that it might actually be the booze that was causing his hair to drop out, as he realized his heavy drinking sessions and his heavy moulting sessions were pretty much coincidental.

He devised an ingenious scientific experiment to

test the theory. He stopped drinking for four hours, and monitored his hair loss with hourly groomings. He lost fifty-seven hairs. Then he repeated the experiment while downing two bottles of whisky. Fifty-three hairs. Conclusive proof, it seemed, that his addiction to alcohol was actually slowing down his hair loss.

The liver was doomed.

Of course, the data could easily have been interpreted in entirely the opposite way. At the time of the experiment, the fifty-seven hairs lost from the first grooming represented almost nine percent of his total stock of six hundred and forty hairs, whereas the second batch of fifty-three hairs represented eleven percent of the remaining five hundred and eighty-three. So, in pure percentage terms, things were speeding up. But Nugent was a man whose scientific principles had long since become compromised by his addictions, and there was no way he was going to question his methodology when it gave such pleasing results.

There's also a distinct possibility, though it can now never be proven, that Nugent may have miscounted the second batch of hair, as he was totally pissed at the time.

All in all, whether you choose to view the facts scientifically or medically, it was a very unsatisfactory situation. Only when the very last hair fell out, and a dear and concerned family friend frog-marched him into a re-hab clinic, did Nugent finally relent. But the damage was done.

Consequently, even at his most relaxed, dozing by the poolside of his Spanish villa many years later, Ted Nugent could easily match the blood pressure of an agitated adult giraffe. But in the current climate of uncertainty, he was likely to blow a gasket at any time. Veins that belonged inside his skull seemed to have sprung up all over the surface, like throbbing worms waiting to explode, and his complexion took its inspiration for exterior décor directly from a beetroot. Little wonder, then, that every time he was punctured in any way, the blood he feared so much squirted out in such a dramatic fashion.

Saturday was turning into a hot, hot, sticky, sticky night, and keeping cool in every sense of the word was going to prove challenging.

Edward was understandably tetchy, because he was suffering from stress, adrenalin fatigue and sleep deprivation. Mr Rogers was tetchy because he had a headache, caused mainly by his nagging wife, Miriam. His nagging wife Miriam was also tetchy because she was suffering with her feet (they had a particular tendency to throb in the heat). Sarah, meanwhile, had acquired a touch of PMT, a strange phenomenon with the capacity to turn an otherwise perfectly reasonable human being into a coiled cobra. Even her dog, not to be outdone, had fleas and couldn't settle. And then there was Nugent, irascible at the best of times, whose blood pressure had recently gone off the scale and whose brains were gradually forcing their way through his skull to form a living, pulsating cycle helmet.

It was going to be a fun evening. All it needed was the addition of a recently reformed smoker, and nothing short of armed riot police could have kept the peace.

In a desperate bid to escape the tense cauldron of the lounge, Edward offered to take Sarah's dog for a quick spin around the block. Sarah was pleased with the offer, and snapped her acceptance immediately.

"Do you want me to come with you?" she asked.

Edward wasn't in the mood for company. He really liked Sarah, or at least the bits of Sarah not currently ravaged by hormones, but right now what he needed most was solitude - time and space to think. Besides, he wasn't sure if she was offering because she really wanted to come, or just to be polite.

"No, it's okay," he replied, and made a bid for the door.

"Edward!" Sarah called after him. A hot, tetchy, stressed and sleep-deprived Edward turned and pounced.

"Please, Sarah, don't complicate things. At the moment I just want to be on my own."

"That's fine by me," replied Sarah. "But if you're taking the dog for a walk, the least you can do is take the dog."

An embarrassed Edward skulked back into the room, scooped the wandering dog lead from the floor, and disappeared into the night.

The way he saw it, he was doing his bit for lounge relations. The removal of one dog and one person would at least help lessen the tension and give the others a slightly better chance of not strangling each other.

Even though Rogers had offered to lend him some old clothes, Edward had chosen to stick with his wife's red trouser suit while out walking the dog, just in case the paparazzi were on the prowl. He figured they wouldn't be looking for a tall, ugly woman with a spaniel - or at least for a tall, ugly and eccentric woman with a joke dog collar. It was just as well. No sooner had Edward rounded the corner than he bumped into a policeman. And when I say bumped into, that's exactly what I mean. Both men had decided to take the inside lane around a blind bend, and Edward managed to catch the unfortunate bobby an absolute pearler with his knee, right in the business end of the groin.

There was the usual delayed reaction, and then the sickening ache welled up inside. The action went something like this.

Policeman: "Huummph!"

Edward: "Oh...." *(quickly switching his voice to fake female falsetto)* "Oh...officer, I'm so sorry."

Policeman: *(now also speaking in falsetto, courtesy of his recently dented undercarriage)* "That's all right, miss. Couldn't be helped. I was just wondering if you've ....Urrggh!"

At which point the policeman jack-knifed into the foetal position and seemed to lose all interest in talking.

What was the policeman about to say? "I was just wondering if you've..." what? Could it be "...seen two men fitting this description?" Was he already hot on their trail? Had they found the stolen car?

Edward had to think on his feet, as he hadn't really got anywhere to sit down. He could do a runner, and hope that the policeman didn't make a miraculous recovery and chase after him. Or he could help him up, stay in character, and bluff his way out of the consequences.

Running away would obviously be far easier - the chances are he'd probably be long gone before the unfortunate bobby even found his feet, let alone the two little dangly things he kept hidden above them. It would, however, arouse unnecessary suspicion, and could possibly result in a major house-to-house search, bloodhounds, helicopters, the drafting in of Tommy Lee Jones and a general escalation of the problem. But then again, sticking around would involve a couple of complications of its own, such as explaining the fact that he was in possession of a transparent animal, and also the reason that he was blatantly not the same sex as his clothes implied.

In the end, he opted for an ingenious compromise. He leant down over the policeman while he was still busy doing an internal audit, and simply asked for permission to leave the scene of the crime.

Edward: *(fake falsetto)* "Officer, I'm so sorry, but I'm about to miss my last bus. Would you mind if I tootled off?"

Policeman: *(enforced falsetto)* "Urrrmph. Off you go, miss. I'll be all right in a minute."

And off he tootled. Thankfully, the rest of the stroll was far less eventful. A few owl hoots, the odd bat, and at one point the peculiar spectacle of a cornered badger facing up to an aggressive dog collar - other than that, nothing much to report.

Edward did a complete circuit of the country lanes surrounding Mr Rogers' cottage - not really knowing where he was going, just turning left wherever he could - and eventually arrived back on familiar territory about half an hour later.

Before returning to the garden, he couldn't resist taking a quick peek around the corner, and was pleased to see that the policeman had eventually found his feet and returned to duty. Either that or he'd died and been removed by a fox.

The evening air was slightly less oppressive now, and Edward felt more relaxed than he had for some considerable time. The walk had done him a power of good.

As he strolled back up the gravel drive past the topiary peacocks, Sarah was outside waiting for him. Luckily, her hormones only worked a ten hour day, and they'd just knocked off for the evening.

"Thanks for doing that," she smiled, as Edward handed back the yapping dog collar.

"No problem," replied Edward. "I needed the air."

"Did he behave himself?"

"I don't know - how can you tell?"

"He didn't tug on the lead or anything?"

"No. Hardly knew he was in there."

"Good boy, Jack!" enthused Sarah, patting the air in front of the collar vigorously.

"Tell me," asked Edward, "are his poos invisible as well?"

"Course they are."

"So, how can you tell if you've trodden in one?"

"The usual way."

"Oh." Edward slumped onto Rogers' garden bench and started sniffing suspiciously at his left shoe.

Sarah looked the other way - up towards the night sky. It was one of those incredibly rare Summer evenings where every single star in the universe was on show. The air was luxuriantly warm and still, and the crickets were out in force, diligently rubbing together their back legs to create the perfect soundtrack.

Sarah sighed with contentment. "Nice evening," she said, somewhat understating the case.

"Yes."

"You look tired."

"Mmm," replied Edward, immediately fighting to stifle a psychosomatic yawn. "I find I need more sleep, the younger I get."

Sarah sat down beside him, her eyes dancing with excitement. "This business of your metabolism. Of getting younger. How does it make you feel?"

"Scared. I've asked Nugent to try and reverse it."

Edward was baffled to see a curious look of shock - almost panic - register on Sarah's face.

"Reverse it? You can't!"

"No, not yet, but he's working on it."

"No, I mean you can't! It's the most fantastic adventure of all time. Why would you want to try and deny it?"

"Perhaps I just want to be normal."

Sarah grabbed his hand. "No. Think it through, Edward."

"I've thought it through."

"Think it through again."

"I've thought it through again. And again. And again. I'm fed up with thinking it through. I just want to be me."

"What does that mean?"

Edward jumped tetchily to his feet and began strutting around, scuffing at the ground with the soles of his shoes.

"I just want to be an ordinary bloke, like I was before. I just want to watch telly, and read the paper, and go to the pub, and…mend pylons, and eat ham sandwiches on Fridays, and… have tie-clips for my birthday, and…" He fizzled out, having thoroughly depressed himself.

"No you don't."

"No I don't. But I don't want this either. I don't know what I want any more."

Sarah glided to his side and put a comforting arm on his shoulder. "Edward, you're at the start of an incredible journey."

"Yeah, well, perhaps I just don't like travelling alone."

"You wouldn't be alone."

"Oh, I'll meet people, I'm sure. Fabulous people. Interesting people. People I could get…"

"Get what?"

Edward's eyes flicked down to the ground. "Very attached to. But…"

Sarah again had to act as prompt. "But what?"

"They'll all be travelling the other way."

Sarah reprised her trademark enigmatic smile. "So what if they're not travelling the other way?"

"What do you mean?"

"Well, like my fruit flies, for example. The human equivalent of 500 years old. They were sort of travelling your way. They could have gone with you."

"Yeah, for a month. Until they exploded."

Sarah removed her arm and started pacing. She had a look on her face - a look Edward knew all too well. It was the same look Nugent was wearing when he was struggling to break the news of Edward's medical predicament. Sarah clearly had something she urgently needed to get off her chest. Edward, meanwhile, had something he urgently needed to get off his shoe.

"Edward..."

"Mmm?"

"I want to tell you something. Edward, are you listening?"

"Mmm."

"Edward, look at me. Stop messing with your shoe."

"How do you get it off if you can't see it?"

"You don't. You buy a new pair."

"Terrific."

"Edward, I want to tell you something. It's an important something. It's even more important than your shoe."

Edward reluctantly diverted his gaze from the offending item. "Go on then."

"In fact it's pretty…mind-boggling."

Edward guffawed privately. After all, when it came to playing host to the bearers of mind-boggling news, he was no wet-behind-the-ears novice, he was the guv'nor.

He was tempted to strut manfully up to Sarah, fix her with his best Humphrey Bogart stare, chuck her playfully under the chin, and say "Cut the health warnings, babe." He might even have added "The problems of two little people don't amount to a hill of beans in this crazy world of ours." But in the end he opted for something slightly less flamboyant, and less to do with hills of beans.

"What the hell. My mind's already boggled."

"But sort of…exciting too."

"What?"

"Don't you think it's weird that…well, just think about what happened to you, and my experiments, and my house exploding, and the fact that we met like this, and, well…it can't all be just coincidence, can it?"

"I don't know. Can it?"

"Edward, I'm a girl who's spent a lot of time with fruit flies."

Edward gave her the look of surprise that a comment like that deserved. "What's that supposed to mean?"

"I get lonely."

Edward's eyes widened. "Are you flirting with

167

me?"

Sarah's face visibly reddened. (To be honest, if it hadn't have done it visibly I probably wouldn't have mentioned it.) "I'm sorry."

"Don't be," said Edward. "I didn't say I minded."

Sarah turned and took a few paces away from the bench. She snatched a large leaf from Rogers' rhododendron and employed it to frantically fan her overheated cheeks.

"I'm embarrassed now."

Edward looked across at her, and suddenly realized for the first time what an outstandingly attractive woman she was. Admittedly, the moon was doing a superb job of her lighting, and the crickets were also doing their bit to enhance the generally romantic atmosphere, but there was something else. There was something indefinably charismatic about her, which I therefore won't attempt to define. Why he hadn't noticed it before he just couldn't imagine. Perhaps he'd just been so preoccupied with his own problems, but it was such a sudden and intense feeling that it rather disorientated him.

In that moment, as she grinned at him through the flapping rhododendron leaf, he knew he'd fallen hopelessly in love with her. It was, without doubt, the most peculiar, unexpected, strangely exciting sensation he had ever experienced, and it had come to him like a bolt from the blue.

Before he'd even had time to check the script, he

heard himself speaking the next line. In the scheme of things, it was fairly inflammatory.

"I get lonely too."

Sarah stopped fanning. "Do you?"

"Oh God, yes."

"Good."

"Oh. Thanks."

"No, I just meant, it's good I'm not the only one getting lonely. It would be quite lonely…getting lonely on your own."

Edward walked slowly towards her. "Earlier on - in there - you said something odd."

"I say a lot of odd things."

"You said 'I knew you'd come.' What did you mean?"

"Look!" Sarah suddenly abandoned the leaf as her hand shot up towards the night sky. "A shooting star!"

Amazingly, Edward's eyes seemed to lock instantly onto the right coordinates, and he saw a dazzling comet chase across the sky. It was ever so slightly surreal - like a Steven Spielberg comet created by an award-winning computer special effects team, and as Edward watched the tail finally sparkle and vanish, he became aware that Sarah was now pressed against his side, her arm linked into his.

The only appropriate word seemed to be "Wow!" and he offered it without hesitation, leaving Sarah to decide if it was inspired by the comet, or her.

"Did you make a wish?" teased Sarah.

Edward squeezed his eyes tightly shut. "Erm…I have now."

"Me too."

"What was yours?"

"Secret. What was yours?"

"Secret."

"Good. That means they'll come true."

"We'll see."

Sarah slid her arm out from his side and headed once again for the rhododendron bush. And once again she had that look on her face, her top teeth tentatively prodding at her bottom lip in preparation for some amazing revelation or other.

Instinctively she plucked another leaf from the bush and began to nervously twiddle with it. Rogers' prize rhododendron was fast becoming a kind of impromptu comfort blanket, and at the rate at which Sarah was taking advantage of its soothing powers there was a distinct possibility that their genial host would wake in the morning to find it stripped to the twigs.

But if the leaf's main role was to help Sarah find the right words, it produced curious results.

"You know, I wouldn't do anything to a fruit fly that I wouldn't do to myself," she said.

Edward replied in the only way that any rational person could reply. "Erm...what do you mean?"

Thankfully, Sarah's follow-up was slightly less cryptic. "There isn't a single one of my longevity experiments that I haven't tried on myself first."

Edward grimaced. "You mean...you've eaten that banana stuff?"

"By the bucket-load. And slept in fields."

"What?"

"Magnetic fields. And I've subjected myself to static charges."

Edward was still convinced that he was in love with this woman. But he was also becoming more convinced by the second that she was, let's say, different, and he made a mental note to leave it a month or so before he took her to meet his parents.

"Er...why?" he asked, not unreasonably.

"To see what happened."

"Oh. Was it worth it?"

"I hoped one day it might be."

"Sounds dodgy to me."

"Oh, I'm used to it," she said casually. "I've been doing stuff like this for over eighty years."

"Nevertheless, you want to be careful you don't...

erm…what did you say?"

Sarah slowly opened her hand. A crushed rhododendron leaf struggled to regain its original shape, but it was too badly damaged. She discarded it and plucked another. "I started experimenting when I was a kid," she added breezily.

"But…you said eighty years."

"Not all my experiments end in disaster, Edward. It's my birthday next month. I'll be eighty-seven years old."

Edward's jaw eventually came to rest on his shoes. Robbed of the power of speech, he shuffled over to the bush and clutched at a handful of leaves. Sarah also took on extra supplies. Rogers' rhododendron was now losing foliage faster than Nugent had lost his follicles, and not a drop of alcohol had passed its roots. A bamboo plant would have had better odds at a Giant Panda eat-as-much-as-you-like restaurant. Sarah sensed that it would be a while before Edward found his tongue again, so she gamely filled time.

"So you see, us meeting like this, well, I think there's more to it than just luck, don't you?"

Edward slowly winched his jaw back into position and had a preliminary crack at using it to make noises.

"Uh…ffufh…ye…ghh…thh…phhh…yuh…you … you're not lying to me?"

"My dear Edward," smiled Sarah. "If a woman

wanted to lie about her age, she wouldn't claim to be eighty-seven."

That was it. Tea with mom and dad was postponed indefinitely. Edward's parents, Tom and Alice (both thankfully still going strong) had always been, let's say, fairly traditional and conservative in their views and lifestyle. They were the backbone of little Britain - the sort that always did the washing on Mondays, the ironing on Tuesdays, had fish on Wednesdays, caught the bus to the supermarket on Thursdays, had a bath on Fridays, cut the lawn on Saturdays, and washed the car on Sundays.

Doing one thing in a day, of course, meant they couldn't possibly contemplate doing a second, and they needed at least seventeen weeks notice to change their routine. Many's the time Edward had offered to take his mom and dad out somewhere, just for a change, only to be told that the offer unfortunately fell on washing day, or lawn-cutting day, or fish-eating day, and therefore had to be declined.

Throughout Edward's wilder teenage years there'd been the usual frictions, of course, as in any household, but he remembered two occasions in particular when he'd incurred his parents' wrath over his controversial choice of girlfriends - once when he took home a Goth, complete with pet bat, and once when he announced that he was dating a girl who was fully three years older than himself. On that evidence, therefore, calmly walking into their bungalow next Sunday and presenting his latest love, an octogenarian witch, might just be pushing his luck.

Edward stared deep into Sarah's eyes. He wasn't quite sure what he was looking for - some sort of answer - but in truth he didn't even understand the question.

It had been an interesting few minutes. He'd fallen madly in love with a woman he'd only just met, and then discovered that she was nearly twice his age. She looked like she was in her late twenties, an age he'd probably look around five years from now. But what would she look like then? It was all a little emotionally confusing.

"So…are you…getting younger too?" squeaked Edward.

"No. Not younger. Just ageing much slower. My appearance has hardly changed at all in the last fifty years."

"But haven't people noticed?"

"I became a recluse a long time ago, Edward. And over the years I've had a few different identities just to keep the civil servants off my back. But on a day-to-day basis it's never been a problem. People are quick to notice change, but they don't seem to be able to notice the lack of it. After all, there's nothing to notice. As far as they're concerned, I'm just the same as I ever was - unremarkable."

"I would never say you're unremarkable."

Sarah grinned. "You know, I think there's an old romantic in there waiting to be unleashed."

"Not so much of the old. In a few years' time I could be a new romantic."

"Mmm…" mused Sarah. "I'm not sure the floppy hair and cape would suit you."

Edward decided to put a late entry of his own into the grinning competition. He couldn't remember the last time he'd felt so at ease with a human being, so mentally in tune. And what a comfort she was. Here, in theory, was someone in exactly the same predicament as the one he was so dreading in the future - the predicament Nugent had warned him about - the dilemma of being psychologically old, but physically young. If it was screwing up Sarah, there seemed to be little evidence of it.

So was the fear at the centre of his decision to reverse the process a gigantic red herring? He had to know.

"So, you're eighty-seven."

"Not until my next birthday. Don't age me."

"But, how do you feel…inside?"

"What - right now?" Sarah took his hand. "Like a teenager. So, I was wondering. If you did decide to go on this incredible journey of yours after all, could I possibly hitch a lift?"

Simple, direct, irresistible.

Sarah smiled and closed her eyes. Even Edward,

not usually a great one for this kind of romantic stuff, sensed that this was his cue to act. And, just in case the moonlight and crickets weren't enough, Rogers added the finishing touch. He'd left his lounge window open on this balmy night, and at that precise moment he chose to slip on one of his favourite Nat King Cole records - opening track, "When I Fall In Love." Only a flashing neon sign above Sarah's head saying "KISS ME NOW" would have strengthened the symbolism.

Edward edged towards her, a tingling bundle of excitement and nerves. Sarah pursed her lips, the moon spot-lit the target area, the world held its breath, Edward crossed his fingers, the crickets crossed their legs, the rhododendron bush prayed for a successful outcome - even Rogers, like some kind of psychic DJ, was already lining up his next favourite track, the Alleluia Chorus from Handel's Messiah. It was a good team effort, and victory seemed assured. So Edward's next move was a slight surprise all round.

He stopped, barely an inch short of her quivering, voluptuous lips, and popped the question. Actually, not *the* question, which might have been considered entirely in keeping with the proceedings, but a somewhat less conventional query.

"What about a wee?"

Sarah, naturally enough, needed a few more details. "Sorry?"

"The dog's wee. Is that invisible as well?"

"Er…yes."

"But it's still wet and warm?"

"Yes, why? Oh, bloody hell! I'm so sorry! Jack, you monster - go away. Sorry, I think he's just jealous. He's used to being the centre of attention."

Had she been in sniffing distance, Edward's wife Mary probably wouldn't have been best pleased to discover that her favourite little red number was now seriously compromised. After all, it was dry clean only. But then again, she probably wouldn't be best pleased to discover that her husband had been wearing it while attempting to snog another woman, so in the overall scheme of things the dog's contribution was a minor one.

Sarah ducked down and began frantically dabbing at Edward's trouser leg with a tissue. It was at this point that Nugent strutted onto the scene. He looked extremely tense and distracted. But then again, he always looked extremely tense and distracted.

"Not interrupting anything, am I?"

"You might have been," replied Edward, "if the dog hadn't got in first."

Luckily, Nugent didn't pursue the point. He wasn't interested. He simply adjusted the settings on his brow to 'maximum furrow' and let rip with a monologue in his best grumpy old man voice.

"Just been watching the BBC News. You'll be glad to know the world's gone completely stark raving mad. Religious leaders are running around like headless chickens claiming you're the devil incarnate, the FBI have just put you on the top of their most wanted list, and a Japanese businessman has just offered a $500 million reward for the first person to successfully extract your DNA."

"Really," replied Edward casually, "and who won the snooker?"

Nugent's brow wasn't in maximum furrow after all. He had a turbo setting which he saved for special occasions. And as if to emphasize his angst, his voice also went down a couple of octaves. He was now Darth Vader in drag. He hadn't sounded this menacing since the old days, when he'd regularly regain consciousness after a heavy drinking session to find that his voice-wave patterns were being picked up by seismologists in neighbouring continents.

"You're not taking this seriously, Edward."

Edward responded with a little more gravitas of his own. "I'm taking this deadly seriously, Ted. And my DNA's staying right where it is, thank you."

Edward's earnest response had an instant effect. Nugent backed off and mellowed. The muscles in his brow gradually came out of contraction, and the furrows began to drop out. Quite where they all went was a mystery. Onlookers couldn't work out why he didn't end up with yards of spare flesh on his head.

Nugent's strut turned into a shuffle. His eye contact faltered.

"Oh, and er…one more thing," he muttered, clutching at a handful of rhododendron leaves. "Your wife's divorcing you."

Edward hadn't seen this one coming, and it winded him. Sarah, too, was stopped in her tracks, and a soggy, crumpled tissue dropped on the floor. She couldn't pretend it was unwelcome news, of course, but she instinctively kept quiet as a mark of respect. There was no verbal response from above, so Sarah slowly stood up, desperately trying to read Edward's facial reaction.

In the absence of anything more inspired, he was tempted to say something like 'What?' But he knew it would have been a redundant and rather pathetic gesture. He'd definitely heard Nugent correctly, and it was hardly the sort of thing he'd joke about. His wife was divorcing him. And he couldn't think of anything to say. So he said nothing.

But the longer he said nothing, the more obvious it became that no-one else was likely to make the next move, and the more awkward the situation became. The rhododendron braced itself for an unprecedented attack. Edward flicked his eyes towards Sarah - just the briefest of glimpses, but enough to know that she was monitoring his soul. Unless all three of them were content to spend the rest of their lives as practising Trappist monks, Edward had to find some words.

He found four. They betrayed no emotional bias, it was just good, solid fact-finding.

"How do you know?" he asked.

"It was on the news," Nugent replied.

And it was at that precise moment that a spirited "Alleluia!" burst forth from Rogers' window.

CHAPTER FIFTEEN

Edward had taken a private moment to reflect on the state of his marriage, or rather lack of it, over by the rhododendron bush, or rather lack of it.

Clearly he was slightly taken aback. Whatever their problems, he and Mary had been together for nearly twenty-five years - they'd shared a house, a bed, a child, a copy of the Radio Times - and to suddenly hear that it was all over from a man who had heard it from another man reading it from an autocue on the BBC News was, to put it mildly, unusual.

Nugent and Sarah, now embarrassed by the length and depth of the silence, exchanged a series of uncomfortable glances and shuffled around in the background. Neither wished to intrude on Edward's private thoughts. Actually, that's not quite accurate. Nugent didn't wish to intrude on Edward's private thoughts. Sarah would have given her right arm to intrude on Edward's private thoughts. At that moment, if there had been tickets available for Edward's private thoughts, the touts could have relieved Sarah of her life savings.

She fought to maintain a dignified silence, but inside it felt like her stomach had fallen into a food blender and her chest cavity had been invaded by a colony of bats.

The mere fact that Edward wasn't a-whooping and a-hollering with unbridled joy wounded her deeply. Never before had she felt such rampant, raging, destructive, green-eyed, good old-fashioned jealousy. But even though it wasn't an emotion she'd ever had any experience of dealing with, she recognized it immediately, and it was all she could do to hold it in check.

Finally, Edward turned and spoke. "Looks like I'm the last to know, then." His tone was measured, calm and neutral. And, much to Sarah's mounting frustration, it did an excellent job of masking whatever he was experiencing inside.

Sarah edged towards him. Flicking her head up and down to avoid direct eye contact, she managed to anaesthetize her feelings just long enough to deliver a polite, formal, and totally pre-fabricated message of sympathy. "I'm sorry, Edward."

Edward's response was a masterstroke.

"Are you?"

Sarah crumpled under the intensive cross-examination. The question - his eyes - demanded an honest answer. Emotion overpowered etiquette, and she immediately shook her head.

"No. No I'm not."

"Oh, well. Probably for the best." Edward's blank neutrality finally melted into a gentle, reassuring smile. "There's only so many tie-clips a bloke can take."

Suddenly, maintaining eye contact was no longer a problem. At that moment, Sarah would have won a staring competition against a barn owl. An embarrassed Nugent tried clearing his throat a few dozen times in a vain attempt to remind them of his existence, but they were oblivious. They'd locked onto each other's eyes like a pair of stubborn rival hypnotists, and began edging closer together. Right on cue, Rogers, the physic DJ, produced his next soundtrack - Tchaikovsky's Romeo and Juliet. This time, surely, the big kiss was inevitable.

But just inches from physical connection, Sarah saw a strange jagged white light flash in Edward's pupils - so bright it caused him to squint and recoil. Before Sarah even had time to turn and establish its source, there was an ominous rumble of thunder. As if scared by the noise, all the house lights trembled momentarily, and then disappeared.

Tchaikovsky's masterpiece ground ignominiously to a halt.

"That's odd," said Sarah, scanning the skies. "It was fine a minute ago."

Sarah's observation was an understatement. It was more than just odd. Suddenly, there was not a single star to be seen, not a cricket to be heard. The evening air was still like soup, but now it was a soup that had gone cold - stodgy, congealed and unappetizing. It was as if the idyllic summer's evening had just been snuffed out by a malevolent giant.

No-one knew quite what was happening, but they knew it wasn't nice. Somehow, the darkness wasn't just physical, it was emotional and psychological. It felt huge, overwhelming, and disturbing. For those informed by religious beliefs, there was an intangible sense of evil in the air.

The eerie, murky silence was pierced by another lightning bolt. This time the thunder crack was instant and deafening, and the rain started to cascade down.

Nugent was stirred into action. Producing a bunch of keys, he tugged at Edward's arm, urging him to follow.

"Come on. Rogers has lent me his car. We need to get back to my lab straight away."

"Why?" asked Edward, resisting the citizen's arrest.

Nugent blurted out his answer like a rescued prisoner who'd just had his gag removed.

"I've been thinking it through, Edward. It took a huge shock to the system to start this. I'm convinced the only way to stop it is another shock of equal magnitude. So, here's what we're going to do. We're going to reproduce exactly the conditions on the day you were struck by lightning. Now, as long as you're not earthed, I reckon I can stick a hundred thousand volts through your spine and you'll survive."

Edward could barely hide his enthusiasm. "No thanks."

"I know it sounds scary, and it will probably blow your eyebrows off, but it's the only way. And we're going to leave nothing to chance. I'll create an electrical field around you to mimic the effect of the pylon. I'll match the temperature and humidity in the lab to the day you were hit. And, even though I'm fairly certain it won't have a direct bearing, just to play safe, I want you to be eating a ham sandwich."

Edward remained unimpressed. "Ted, no."

Nugent forcefully grabbed Edward's sleeve and wheeled him round. Had it been a seedy bar, and had Nugent been drunken stranger, Edward might instinctively have swung for him. But it wasn't a seedy bar, and Nugent wasn't a drunken stranger. Just an agitated and concerned friend demanding his undivided attention.

"Listen to me, Edward," pleaded Nugent. "It's not just the paparazzi now - it's the FBI, private detectives, pharmaceutical companies, religious nuts, ruthless bounty hunters, rich Japanese loonies, and loonies who are neither rich nor Japanese - it's only a matter of time before one of them hunts you down."

"He's right, Edward," said Sarah. "They'd never leave us alone."

All this time, their dialogue was being neatly punctuated by the flashes and bangs of a spectacular horror movie storm. As with all good horror movie storms, it performed as if it were written into the script - perfectly choreographed with the action, never crashing over an important word, always waiting for the appropriate gaps between lines to deliver its menacing interjections.

Another huge crackle of energy sizzled through the air, and Nugent moved centre stage. "We need to reverse this, Edward, before the vultures descend and tear you to shreds. Let's cure you now, and send them away empty-handed. It's the only way to make them stop."

Edward glanced at Sarah, then back to Nugent. They perfectly symbolized the choice he had to make. Would he be ruled by the heart, or the head? The storm waited patiently in the wings, studying the script, ready to deliver its next line.

"I don't want to be cured."

Cue lightning and thunderbolt. It was a blistering delivery. Just yards from the main players, Rogers' rhododendron bush took the full impact of a spectacular strike, and was instantly set alight.

All in all, it was turning out to be an impressive performance from the forces of darkness. The burning bush motif was a particularly cheeky and inspired ad-lib, and had there been a London Agent in the audience, the storm might well have been offered a three-year contract.

But despite the drama of the lightning strike, it was Edward's previous statement that had sent Nugent reeling.

"What? But you…"

"I've changed my mind, Ted. I want to stay as I am."

Sarah smiled another one of her private smiles. She must surely by now have had one of the biggest private collections of smiles in the country. One day, perhaps, they would all finally be put on show in a public gallery, and she'd be fondly remembered as a Cheshire cat.

Nugent, like all of them, was now completely drenched to the skin. It was as if the rain had forgotten it was supposed to fall in inches, and had decided to go for metres instead.

Even without the added drama of thunderclaps, the noise level was now becoming extraordinary, as raindrops ricocheted off the roof of Rogers' greenhouse like the bullets of a thousand tiny machine guns.

Water was dripping relentlessly from the end of Nugent's nose, eyelashes, chin and ears as he stood in front of Edward. At least the other two had hair to help soak up deluge. Nugent needed guttering around his brow. But for some reason it never for one moment occurred to any of them to go indoors.

Nugent put his hands on Edward's shoulders and gave him his most earnest, concerned stare.

"Edward, we talked about this…"

Edward nodded. "I know," he said. "But things have changed."

"What things?"

Edward flicked his eyes over towards Sarah. "I'm not going to be alone any more."

Sarah paddled alongside Edward and squeezed his hand. Nugent seemed to adopt the demeanour of a betrayed wife. "What's going on?"

"It's a long story," said Edward.

"Eighty years long," Sarah added, cryptically.

The storm, having dutifully waited for all the quieter and more delicate dialogue to finish, now once again flexed its muscles in spectacular fashion. And this time, mixed in with the bangs of the thunder, was the noise of an approaching police siren.

"My God!" screamed Nugent. "They're on to us already. Come on."

Edward stood firm. "No. You go."

Nugent wheeled round so quickly it sent a trail of spray spiralling out from his brow, like liquid sparks from a catherine wheel. "Edward, you don't know what you're letting yourself in for."

"I don't care," replied Edward - not in a petulant way, but calmly, resolutely and with total sincerity. "We'll get through it together. Go on - really, you go, we'll be fine."

"But...I can't just leave you. Not now."

"Ted, you could stay forever and I still could never thank you enough for everything you've done for me. You've been amazing. Really. Inspirational. And a true friend. In fact, my only friend. But I've made my mind up. I'll take my chances in the future. This is what I want. I know that now. I didn't before. But I do now."

Nugent was many things, but he was not stupid, and he was not insensitive. Even the most thick-skinned salesman would have realized that Edward was not about to change his mind. Nugent squelched his way slowly back to them, and manfully shook Edward's hand, relieving his sleeve of about a gallon of water in the process.

"Good luck," said Nugent. "You'll need it." He turned to Sarah and smiled - or at least Nugent's equivalent of a smile, which was a sort of light-hearted scowl. "And as for you..."

Sarah stroked her finger gently across Nugent's cheek to remove the excess moisture, and then planted a tender little kiss right in the centre.

"You're a good man, Ted Nugent."

It was hard to tell if Nugent actually blushed. His high blood pressure over many years had made his cheeks so ruddy that it would take a well calibrated spectrometer to pick up the difference. But he did give a tell-tale little cough before proceeding. "You do realize, young lady, that you've got someone very special here, don't you?"

"Oh, yes," she replied, beaming. "Yes. I do."

"Well, just…erm…just look after him for me."

"I will." Sarah leaned forward and whispered in his ear. "And don't worry, I'll never tell anyone what I saw up your skirt."

"Cheeky."

Just like the storm, the wailing police sirens had waited for the main messages to be delivered before cranking up the volume.

"Go on," urged Edward. "You don't want to be caught up in all of this. It's me they're after."

Nugent nodded silently. Enough had been said. He paddled silently away into the night.

Edward gently released his hand from Sarah's grip and moved towards the rhododendron. It had not been a good night for the bush. Stripped of its leaves by insecure bystanders, it had then been decimated by a thunderbolt of epic proportions. For that brief moment at least, it had provided an awe-inspiring spectacle, but now that the rain had doused the flames it was in a sorry state. Just a few blackened, brittle sticks, smoking in the mud.

Edward crouched down on his knees to examine the cremated remnants and pay his last respects. He understood. He'd been there. Who knows - perhaps from that moment on the bush would start to get younger.

A family of frogs, who had been happily sheltering under the bush until it disintegrated, came out of their state of shock and temporary blindness and made a bid for high ground to escape the deluge. They liked water as much as the next amphibian, but Sunday was their day off, and enough was enough. Their sudden movement made Sarah jump, which in turn made Edward jump. He might in turn have made the frogs jump, had they not already been ahead of the game.

Shooting stars, burning bushes, raging floods, a plague of frogs - it had been a night of strangely familiar symbolism. What the symbols symbolized, of course, was quite another matter. He'd leave that to a higher power.

Edward brushed the charcoal from his fingers and looked up at Sarah. "You're good at all this mystical stuff. Tell me - is it bad luck to talk about a wish after it's come true?"

"I don't think so," replied Sarah.

"Because I think mine just did."

"Mine too."

"Right," said Edward. "So what was yours?"

"Oh, I wished for the bush to set fire," she replied mischievously. "You?"

"To be scared by a frog."

They grinned childishly at each other. Edward stood up and closed his arms around her waist. "You realize we're going to be more famous than the Beckhams?"

"Yes," beamed Sarah. "But hopefully with an even longer shelf life."

"And less tattoos," added Edward.

"Ah," said Sarah. "Don't be so sure about that."

She wriggled from his grip and turned, lifting up her T-shirt to reveal the base of her spine. The light wasn't good, but Edward could just make out the detail of a small but extraordinary tattoo. It was the classic, simple arrow and heart motif, flanked by two names. Sarah, and Edward.

"How the bloody hell…you are a witch!"

"Not really. Just a drunken moment with an old boyfriend, years and years ago. He broke my heart. It has made me rather picky about my relationships ever since though. They have to be tall, dark, handsome…"

"And called Edward."

"Precisely. You see? I knew you'd come."

Edward smirked an uncontrollable smirk. "Sarah Appleby, you are one weird and wonderful lady."

She eyed up the person stood before her. Six feet tall, two days' stubble and wearing a red trouser suit. "And so, my dear, are you."

"You should see me in my bikini," he added drily.

I use the word drily in a purely figurative sense, of course, given that he was extremely wet. Actually, a bikini would have been a far better choice of attire for Edward at that moment, because swimming was fast becoming the only means of transport. The worst of the storm seemed to have passed over, but so much rain had fallen in the last twenty minutes that the country lanes had become streams, the streams had become rivers, the rivers had burst their banks, and the neighbouring fields had become lakes.

Luckily, Rogers' cottage was on relatively high ground, and they'd escaped with nothing more serious than a power cut and an impromptu garden makeover - the flower beds were transformed into a natural water feature, the lawn was a paddy field, the shed boasted its own moat, and the gravel drive was now an excellent spot for trout tickling. Others, though, would not be so lucky, and the insurance companies were no doubt already planning a strategy to deal with the temporary hit on their profits. It would be the usual strategy, of course. Doubling the premiums of everyone, except the ones they refused to cover at all. God forbid that insurance should ever be an industry subject to risk.

In an attempt to at least synchronize their swimming, Sarah took both of Edward's hands in hers. "So, are you ready?" she said.

"What for?" asked Edward.

"For the incredible journey of life."

"Let's see now…erm…" Edward suddenly bent down, plucked her feet from the mud, lifted her up and cradled her tightly in his arms. "Yep. All packed."

"Mmm. Big strong boy."

"Oh, this is nothing," replied Edward. "You should see me in ten years' time."

"I'll look forward to it. Well?"

"Well what?"

"Give us a kiss, then," grinned Sarah.

"No way. You're old enough to be my mother."

"Don't knock it. One day I might have to be."

At that moment, power was restored to the cottage. The lights flickered on, and the theme to Romeo & Juliet whirred back into life. Their heads were now just centimetres apart. Their eyes were locked together. Surely, surely this time, nothing could come between them.

And nothing did. Their lips met, and for a brief, electrifying moment they were as one.

Romeo and Juliet.

The ultimate love story.

The ultimate tragedy.

What happened next was not for the faint-hearted.

CHAPTER SIXTEEN

For that brief, precious moment, their souls had touched and intertwined. Now, violently and without warning, they were ripped apart.

Edward stood in a state of numb confusion. Just seconds ago he'd been holding Sarah in his arms - he was actually kissing her. Yes, kissing her - he was sure he hadn't dreamt it. Now, in the flick of a switch, the ecstasy had become agony. Suddenly there was nothing but chaos, pain and shrill madness. Sarah had recoiled from his lips with a sickening squeal and slumped lifelessly to the floor. Had she been shot? Had she been struck by lightning?

A huge surge of adrenalin kicked Edward out of his daze. He knelt down beside her, his heart thumping ferociously out of his chest, and carefully lifted her mud-spattered head from the ground, anxiously scanning for any sign of a wound.

"Sarah? What's wrong? What happened?"

She was still conscious, but deathly pale - and clearly just as bewildered as Edward. Her voice was frail and trembling, but clear and coherent. "I don't know. Nothing. Just…just some sort of weird stomach cramps. I think I'm okay n…arrgh!"

For the second time in seconds, Sarah was wrenched from Edward's grasp by a gigantic involuntary spasm. But this time the agony was unyielding. Her body twitched and jerked helplessly in the mud, as if her spinal cord was being perpetually jabbed by a giant electric cattle prod.

Edward watched in awe and utter despair as she lay writhing and splashing on the ground, arching her back, cruel, cruel pain wracking her body, gasping, screaming for help.

But the horror was only just beginning. Sarah's stomach was beginning to swell up like a gigantic inflating balloon.

"Help me!" she screamed.

Edward, paralyzed with fear and panic, grabbed her hand and screamed back at her. "What can I do? Tell me what to do!"

Another huge spasm jolted through her body, violently expelling the air from her lungs and leaving her unable to respond. Her abdomen was now so vilely distended that it had torn through her sodden t-shirt. And still it grew, a few more inches every second, tearing muscles and sinews as it went. Sarah's skin was now stretched to the point of transparency. Edward could see the internal organs and veins pulsating inside.

From somewhere, Sarah found the strength to speak. "I'm sorry Edward. I don't…think…I'm going to be able to go with you after all."

Edward was now sobbing uncontrollably. "No…you can't do this to me, Sarah. You can't leave me on my own. I can't go through this without you. Do you hear me? Sarah!"

Sarah put her hand up to Edward's mouth and touched it tenderly to quieten his panic. And then, as if to instinctively ensure that it remained his lasting memory of her, she summoned up one final, frail, utterly captivating smile.

"Look after Jack for me, will you?" she said.

And at that moment, her torso exploded into a yellow mist.

Edward didn't hear the sickening thud. He didn't feel the vile, sticky yellow liquid now cascading down, coating his face and body. His world had become silent, disconnected, surreal, and in slow-motion.

As the energy fell from Sarah's eyes, he gently laid her head onto the ground, and stroked the excess water from her face. From somewhere deep inside the silence came the distant echoing sound of a voice. His own voice. "Sarah?" he whispered. "Sarah?"

But Sarah did not respond. Sarah was dead. And as he looked down at her body, the protective membrane of numb, silent shock was suddenly pierced, and ugly sounds began to seep in.

A blistering lightning bolt announced the unwelcome return of the lightning storm, now back for a spectacular encore. But this time, it was even more devastating and destructive than before - splitting trees and ear drums in one strike, cracking open roofs, fracturing roads, lashing all in its wake like the whip cracks of an angered God.

From the eerie silence of a few moments ago, Edward now found himself subjected to the most terrifying and unrelenting onslaught of noise. Menacing thunder, howling wind, rain battering and clattering its way down to the ground. And for the first time, Edward could now hear his own screams. They were screams of pure fear.

Hard on the heels of the noises, came the feeling of despair. Total, black, empty, despair. It flooded in, drowning his senses. Edward could feel himself being sucked into a deep, desolate vortex. It was like emotional quicksand, slowly pulling him in, suffocating his soul.

In a last gasp bid for freedom, Edward leapt up, tossing back his head, brandishing his fists and screaming his defiant anger to the skies. "No!!!!"

And that's when he saw it.

The first time it was nothing more than subliminal - a ghostly image printed on his mind by a flash of light, an image which had no time to develop. But moments later came the confirmation. There it was, in the neighbouring field, surreally silhouetted for several shuddering seconds against the flickering night sky.

A deeply flustered Mr Rogers, armed with a huge umbrella and Wellington boots, emerged from the cottage just in time to see Edward trudging down the drive. He called anxiously after him, asking if he was all right, and what had happened to the others.

But Edward did not turn. It was unlikely at that moment that he was capable of hearing anything above the deafening roar of his own thoughts.

He was heading for the epicentre of the storm. And he wanted the best vantage point he could find.

CHAPTER SEVENTEEN

No-one was seriously expecting to pull Edward from the manure alive and, as the charred and stinking body was eventually unearthed, the paramedic on standby to give mouth-to-mouth was keeping his fingers crossed that it wasn't even a close call.

It wasn't.

As Detective Inspector Thompson leant over to examine the body, a young policewoman came bounding over the field. She pushed her way through the small crowd of interested bystanders who were braving the elements and ducked under the police tape that cordoned off the bottom of the pylon.

"Right, sir," she said, enthusiastically brandishing a notebook. "His name's Edward Jones. He worked for the Utilities company."

"What the hell was he doing up there on a day like this?" snarled Thompson.

"Well, whatever it was, sir, it wasn't official. He was suspended from work last month following health problems."

"What sort of health problems?"

"Severe depression, mainly, and some delusional stuff. I spoke to his wife. Well, ex-wife - she was divorcing him. She says she hadn't been able to get through to him for months. He seemed to be locked away in his own world."

Thompson stuffed his hands deep into his pockets and circled the body. "Anything from his doctor?"

"Nothing official. He refused to see his own GP, claiming she was trying to stab him in the buttocks."

"What?"

"He told his wife he was seeing another doctor, but she never found out who. He was also convinced he was being hounded by the paparazzi, he stole his neighbour's car, he attacked a tramp in the park while wearing his wife's clothes…"

"In a nutshell, DC Jarvis, you're telling me he's a total fruitcake."

"Don't know about fruit cake, sir - possibly a fruit fly."

"Fruit fly?"

"He once said something to his wife about being a human fruit fly."

"Bloody hell. What goes on in the dark recesses of the mind, eh?"

"I've haven't got to the best bit yet, sir. His wife

also says she once caught him - are you ready for this, sir? - talking to an imaginary dog."

Inspector Thompson clearly wasn't ready for this. "Imaginary bloody dog?"

"A spaniel."

"How the hell did she know it was a spaniel?"

"I suppose she had to take his word for it, sir."

Thompson thought this seemed as good a time as any to light up his next cigarette. It was, after all, a good eleven minutes since his last cigarette, and not all of his call-outs had the luxury of being outdoors. He disappeared inside his coat to protect his lighter from the wind and rain, and re-appeared a few moments later shrouded in a puff of blue smoke.

"Puts my problems into perspective, I suppose."

"What problems have you got, sir?"

"Right now, a dead body and a lot of paperwork."

DC Jarvis peered for the first time at Edward's blackened face. "Weird expression, sir."

"That, DC Jarvis, is fear. Pure and simple."

"Shame. Good-looking chap, too."

"If you say so," said Thompson, slightly churlishly. "And not very old, by the look of him."

"That's the irony of it all, sir. His wife reckons that that's what's behind all this."

"How do you mean?"

"Well, apparently, he was totally obsessed by the whole idea of growing old. It completely freaked him out. She said he went berserk when he first discovered a bald spot. Took pictures of it and everything. I've got one here his wife found."

She handed Thompson a crumpled Polaroid. He screwed up his eyes, moving the photograph in and out, struggling to make sense of it.

"What the hell's this?"

"His head, sir. Bald patch."

"Really? Must get my eyes tested. Stick it in a plastic bag."

"I suppose he just became more and more agitated as he got towards the big day."

"Big day?" said Thompson. "What do you mean?"

"Well, I don't think it's any coincidence he did this today, sir. It was his birthday tomorrow. He would have been forty."

Thompson rolled his eyes with all the irony of a man who viewed forty with fond nostalgia rather than imminent dread.

"Isn't life supposed to start at forty?"

DC Jarvis grinned. "I'll let you know, sir."

"How old are you, Jarvis?"

"Twenty-seven, sir. Twenty-eight next week."

"Now you've depressed me."

"Why, sir?"

"I was twenty-seven, twenty-seven years ago."

A mischievous smile flashed across her face. "Well, your eyes might be dodgy, sir, but at least your mind's still sharp. I couldn't have worked that out so quickly."

"Don't be cheeky..."

"Oh, excuse me, sir. My mobile."

"What about it?"

"It's ringing."

"Bugger. Does this mean I'm going deaf as well?"

"No, sir. I've got it on silent vibrate."

"Oh. Enjoy."

The young policewoman plucked the phone from her jacket and respectfully moved a few paces away to answer it.

DI Thompson crouched once again over the blackened body of Edward Jones, shaking his head in disbelief. He'd bumped into some nasty customers in his time - interviewed his fair share of murderers, rapists, psychopaths, the seriously deranged - he'd tidied up plenty of murder victims too, and never had any trouble whatsoever remaining professionally detached. But there was something about the charred figure before him which touched his heart. The blackened face had captured a moment of pure terror. It reminded Thompson of some of the figures he'd seen on holiday in Vesuvius last year - their moment of fear frozen for all time. Okay, so this was probably just another nutter who'd lost the plot and found a novel way to top himself. But whatever spectres had driven him to do it were real enough to Edward Jones. And lady luck had hardly been on his side. Most people would die of old age waiting to be struck by lightning. He managed it first time, on cue.

"Poor sod," Thompson growled, quietly. "What was scaring you so much, eh?"

He went to take another drag from his cigarette, but there was nothing left but a blackened filter. The fierce wind had accelerated the burning process, leaving Thompson with no moral alternative but to light another. As he stubbed the dog-end into the muddy ground, he spotted something encrusted into Edward's left hand. He uncurled the body's stiffened fingers and liberated it, just as DC Jarvis returned to his side.

"What's that, sir?"

Thomson sniffed at the cremated specimen. "Ham toasty."

"No time for lunch, sir. We've been called to another incident."

"Where?"

"Grange Common. Sarah Appleby's place."

"Oh, what now? Neighbours reported seeing flying broomsticks again?"

"Something a bit more substantial this time, sir. Her house has exploded."

"Good God. Any casualties?"

"So far, just a crow. But it was a bit of a nasty one, sir. We've no idea yet if Sarah was in there. If she was, well…she's going to take some finding."

"All right - get moving. I'll tidy up here and meet you over there."

The young policewoman was just ducking under the police cordon when she was called back.

"DC Jarvis?"

"Sir?"

DI Thompson was crouching down, staring intently at the body. "Do you ever worry about getting old?"

"Can't say I've really thought about it, sir."

"What would scare you enough…to do this to yourself?"

"Dunno, sir. Certainly not a few wrinkles."

She turned once more to leave, but something made her stop. The question had deserved more respect, more thought. It had deserved an answer, and from nowhere one had suddenly occurred to her.

"Actually, sir…the thing that would probably scare me most…well, it's not the getting old, is it, sir? It's being on your own. Not having anyone to share it with. I think that would get to me."

Thompson stared at her, absorbing the thought, then slowly looked down at the ground. Huge raindrops were beating circles into the muddy puddles around his feet. He was drenched to the skin, and a little involuntary shudder went through his body. He slowly nodded. "Mmm. Okay, go on."

He glanced up, expecting her acknowledgment, but she had already gone. In fact, she was already way across the field, busily dispersing the bystanders in the distance. He must have been deep in thought for longer than he'd realized.

Thompson instinctively pulled his left hand to his mouth, only to find himself sucking on the remnants of a blackened ham toasty. He removed it with the sort of haste you'd remove other unwelcome objects from your mouth, such as a slug, or a pair of fornicating cockroaches, and studied the foreign object in the palm of his hand.

Good job it wasn't a major piece of evidence in a murder trial, he thought. He'd have buggered up the DNA good and proper. Imagine if it came out in court, during intense cross-examination of an expert witness, that the saliva samples found on the murder weapon had been traced back to the investigating officer, who had accidentally put it in his mouth and sucked on it.

DI Thompson furtively looked around, tossed the charred food into the long grass below the pylon, and turned to signal to his colleagues to bring on the body bag.

As the food landed, there was a grateful bark from a small, hungry dog.

At least, that's how it sounded.

Thompson turned to look, but there was nothing there.

"Now I'm bloody hearing things," he muttered.

As he began the long, muddy trek across the field to his car, DC Thompson lit another cigarette. He knew it was bad for him, but what the hell. His wife had left him last year, he had no children, his parents were dead, and he had no real friends to speak of - he was a policeman, for God's sake. So it was no longer anyone's business but his own how he chose to abuse his body.

In the absence of any meaningful willpower, he'd long since adopted the basic philosophy that it was pointless denying himself life's small pleasures, in return for the uncertain promise of a longer life, without life's small pleasures.

Live for the day, that was his new motto. And if he could live for several days, that was a bonus. 'Carpe diem' the Romans had called it. He'd learnt that on holiday last year. Seize the moment. After all, who knows what's around the corner? Tomorrow, he could be run over by a bus.

Tomorrow, he could be struck by lightning.